7/00

Our Only
May Amelia

Our Only
May Amelia

by Jennifer L. Holm

HarperCollins*Publishers*

Map drawn by Elissa Della Piana
Photographs on pages xvi, 186, and 236 from the collection of Pacific County
Historical Society: PCHS #5-19-90.1.11, PCHS #1998.57.1, PCHS #1996.83.12.
Photographs on pages 42 and 172 courtesy of Archive Photos. Photographs on pages
ii, 108, and 224 courtesy of Timothy Hampson. Other photographs from the
private collections of Jennifer L. Holm and Nicholas Krenitsky.
Special thanks to Barry Leo Delaney.

Library of Congress Cataloging-in-Publication Data
Holm, Jennifer L.
    Our only May Amelia / by Jennifer L. Holm.
        p.   cm.
    Summary: As the only girl in a Finnish American family of seven brothers, May
Amelia Jackson resents being expected to act like a lady while growing up in
Washington state in 1899.
    ISBN 0-06-027822-6. – ISBN 0-06-028354-8 (lib. bdg.)
    [1. Frontier and pioneer life—Washington (State)—Fiction. 2. Brothers and sisters—
Fiction. 3. Sex role—Fiction. 4. Finnish Americans—Fiction.
5. Washington (State)—Fiction.] I. Title.
PZ7.H732226Ou 1999   98-47504
[Fic]—dc21   CIP
                                                                    AC

Typography by Alison Donalty   5 6 7 8 9 10   ❖   First Edition

*For my mother and father
and
for my grandfather Michael Hearn,
who told me to follow my heart.*

ACKNOWLEDGMENTS

A lot of research went into the telling of this tale. Most of that research came straight from my dad, William Wendell Holm, M.D., and his Long Memory. And it is priceless.

For additional research assistance many thanks to: Elizabeth Holm for her meticulous archiving of pioneer life in the Naselle River Valley; Louise Hunter and Mitzi Hunter for their Finnish-American culinary knowledge; Bruce Weilepp and the Pacific County Historical Society and Museum for terrific photo and historical research; local Naselle historian Carlton Appelo; and Louise Espy and Wede Espy, for paving the way with *Oysterville*.

I have been most fortunate to have friends and colleagues who supported my writing. For their support and good advice I'd like to thank: Sara Cleary-Burns; Stanley Burns, M.D.; Alvin Calderon; Paul Najjar; Ruth Cruz; Adam Cruz; Arpad Baksa; Mitch Galin; my attorney, Joel Shames; and Helenrae Grover.

And special thanks to: my editor Ginee Seo for her insightful editing; the whole gang at HarperCollins, especially Kelsey Stevenson for her patience and Emily Hahn for her good humor; my terrific agent, Jill Grinberg, for her wise guidance; Jill Siegel for her great support and friendship; Wendy Wilson, who laughed out loud when she read the manuscript; my mentor Ralph Slotten for his quiet encouragement; my brothers Jonathan and Matthew Holm for their great support; and most of all to my sweet husband for his excellent suggestions, love, and ability to put up with me and my cat.

Last but not least, many thanks to my mom, Penny Holm, who told me to Pay Attention.

TABLE OF CONTENTS

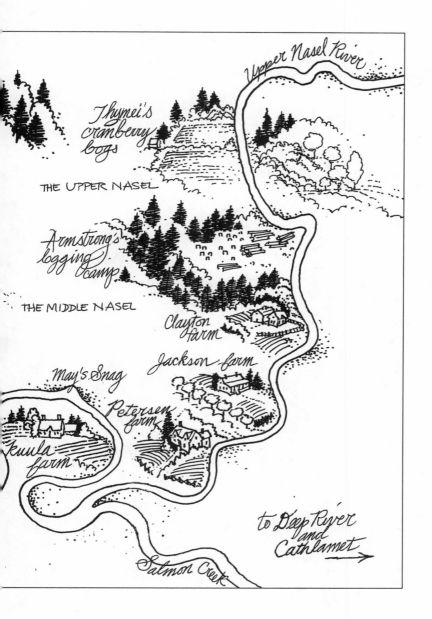

Upper Nasel River

Thymei's cranberry bogs

THE UPPER NASEL

Armstrong's logging camp

THE MIDDLE NASEL

Clayton farm

Jackson farm

May's Snag

Petersen farm

Kuula farm

to Deep River and Cathlamet →

Salmon Creek

If you don't go, you can't return.
—Finnish proverb

Our Only
May Amelia

CHAPTER ONE

My Brother
Wilbert Tells Me

My brother Wilbert tells me that I was the first
ever girl born in Nasel, that I was A Miracle. He
tells me this as we stand at the edge of the water,
on the Nasel River, watching it rush by crazily. He
is trying to cheer me up.

Wilbert has found me here on the Baby Island
where I have run away on account of Pappa being
awful to me. Even Wilbert says it is terrible that
Pappa was awful to me today, on my own birthday.
Wilbert is thirteen and my favorite brother which
is something indeed since I have so many brothers, more than any girl should have. My secret
birthday wish is to get a sister but I don't know
how likely that is.

These are my brothers:

Matti is eighteen.

Kaarlo is seventeen and one half and is really our cousin but I guess he's sort of a brother.

Isaiah is sixteen.

Wendell is fifteen.

Alvin is fourteen.

Ivan is fourteen too. He is Alvin's twin and they look as alike as two blackberries. Only Wilbert and I can tell them apart, even Mamma has trouble.

Wilbert is thirteen.

May Amelia Jackson is twelve. That is Me.

We live on the Nasel in the state of Washington. It is 1899.

Pappa is always yelling at me Don't Get Into Mischief May Amelia when all I'm ever doing is what some other boy has done first. He says that I am a Girl and because I am a girl I cannot be doing what the boys are doing, that there is danger everywhere. Wilbert tells me that Pappa has had a Hard Life. That you can see the hardness in the lines of his face, what with coming all the way to Washington after being pressed into the Finnish Navy and leaving Finland. That's why he's hard on me. But Wilbert's wrong. Pappa doesn't like little girls very much in general, and me in particular.

Mamma has a baby in her belly and Pappa said

Children I sure do hope your mamma gives us another boy 'cause I don't think I can stand another May Amelia. He said this in front of all the boys, after hollering at me for going up to Ben Armstrong's logging camp by myself. I said But Ivan and Alvin go up by themselves and he said May Amelia, I will not abide any arguments.

But Pappa— I said.

Then he hollered so loud I'm sure they heard him over at the Petersen farm.

That logging camp's a dangerous place for a young girl! he hollered. I don't want you running around there, Do You Hear Me? Then his eyebrows got all fierce-looking and met in the middle and he shook his finger at me and That Was That.

I hate it when he scolds me so I ran away. I took the little rowboat onto the Nasel and went to the Baby Island and hid in the old sorcerer tree until Wilbert came to fetch me home. He's the only one who knows about the sorcerer tree. It's all hollow-like and fits a small child like me just fine.

I say Wilbert I reckon I would like to be buried in the sorcerer tree when I die, and he says Fine May but you're not likely to die anyways. You're only twelve and you hafta to be old to die didn't you know that?

I say I did but was just a-planning.

And now Wilbert is fooling around with Bosie, trying to get Bosie to jump into the water and chase after the little fishies. Bosie's a scruffy dog. His hair is missing in places from where it's been lost in fights with the mean raccoon who lives behind the milking barn.

It is starting to get hot, it being nearly June, and here on the Nasel the breeze is hiding, and the mosquitoes are trying to bite me the way Bosie is trying to bite the little fishies in the water. Bosie's a strong swimmer but the Nasel is rough, and the water is dragging him downstream.

Wilbert, I say. Fetch Bosie out before he washes into the Shoalwater Bay.

The Nasel runs into the Shoalwater Bay farther downstream and then into the wide ocean. To the south overland is the mighty Columbia River, and on the other side of the Columbia is Oregon and Astoria. Astoria is the only real city in these parts and it's a wicked place full of shanghaiers and sea-men and all sorts of fancy folks, not like out here in Nasel where the only fancy thing is a new pair of shoes. At least that's what Wilbert tells me—I have never been there myself. Our Aunt Alice lives there and she is very fancy indeed. She is coming to visit on account of my birthday, and so are my

Aunt Feenie and Uncle Henry. I am turned twelve this very day and I have spent most of it hiding in a tree.

Wilbert whistles for Bosie.

Bosie is not a very good fisherdog. He has caught one fish only, and a small one at that, not enough even for a small child's supper. When he gets out of the water he shakes his scruffy fur and gets Wilbert all wet.

Stop It Bosie! Wilbert yells.

Wilbert scowls fiercely and the scar crinkles under his eye from where Kaarlo decked him in a fight.

Let's try and fish, I say. We can get some salmon and surprise Mamma.

Now that Mamma has a baby in her belly she is worn out all the time so I have to help her a lot around the house with the cooking and just about everything. That is why I hope the new baby will be a girl. Then all the hard work will be worth it.

Not to mention I sure am tired of being the only girl around here.

The Baby Island is a very small island in the middle of the Nasel River down from our farm. When I was a small child, I used to believe it was where all the babies came from on account of its name. It's a good place for fishing even though it is where the Chinooks bury their dead. I have never seen a dead Indian here but I expect they keep them hid. Those Indians sure are clever.

Wilbert swears to me that the Baby Island is accursed on account of the Chinook spirits that wander there but I think he is only just scared and he calls things names when he is scared of them. He tells me our teacher Miss McEwing is a Witch and she is the most loveliest woman I have ever seen. Why she is sweet and nice and kind to us children, not at all like old Mr. Barton who used to whip our hands with pine branches. No indeed. Miss McEwing even lets us take off our wet clothes and sit by the potbelly stove to dry off when the weather is bad which is almost always it seems.

Wilbert doesn't like studies and cannot speak English very well, only Finnish, and Miss McEwing is always correcting him, saying Speak English Wilbert Jackson. Mamma says all us children must learn to speak English or else we will always have trouble even though she and Pappa speak mostly Finnish. Nearabout everyone around here speaks Finnish. Our real last name is Juntilla, but when Pappa came over from Finland, they said

6

it would be better for him if he had an American name and that is why we are Jacksons.

Wilbert has a hard time with the English and one time he peeked at my answer sheet when Miss McEwing was clear across the room looking the other way. No Wandering Eyes Wilbert Jackson, she said and ever since then Wilbert has been convinced that Miss McEwing is a Witch.

Even though Wilbert gets scared it is okay because he is only afraid of Miss McEwing and the Chinook spirits on the Baby Island. Nothing else scares him, not even Pappa's belt. He has come all the way to the Baby Island which he thinks is cursed to find me, May Amelia, a no-good girl.

I have plenty of brothers but only one Wilbert.

We go to the part of the island where the water is slow, where the fishies are fat and lazy. The breeze blows gently here and I think it is not a bad thing after all to be spending my birthday fishing with Wilbert. There is nothing I like better.

My line is in the water and right away it seems I feel a tug. The line tugs hard and I tug back. A salmon's silky fin slip-slides in the water.

I got one Wilbert! I yell.

Hold on May, he says and drops his own line

7

and runs over. He helps grab the pole but the salmon is strong. It's pulling hard and Bosie's barking and barking and then all of a sudden Bosie jumps into the water and bites my fish.

Bosie Let Go! Wilbert and I say together.

But dumb ole Bosie has caught only the hook. The fish who is smarter than our dog has gotten away. Bosie's yelping and whining on account of the hook that's stuck in his cheek. Wilbert dives right into the Nasel, clothes and all, and brings Bosie back to shore.

He is a sad dog indeed by the time Wilbert drops him on the bank.

Hold him down May, Wilbert says. I gotta take the hook outta his cheek.

Bosie's plenty mad—the hook must hurt terribly—but still I hold him down. Wilbert just sticks his hand right into Bosie's mouth and pries the hook out. Bosie's bleeding, but he's happy to have the hook out of his mouth. He yelps and licks Wilbert's face.

You sure are a dumb dog Bosie, Wilbert says.

We live in a valley on a homestead along the Nasel. Our land snakes from high upriver near Ben Armstrong's logging camp right down to a bay by our house, where we have a small dock so that a body can tie up a rowboat which is very handy indeed. There are big fat mountains to the north full of tall pine trees and all sorts of Chinook secrets. Our farm has cows and sheeps and pigs and a fat barn cat named Buttons. We make milk and sell it and the cream too to the Sunshine Mill downriver.

Aunt Alice is at the house when we get home. She has come all the way from Astoria on account of my birthday. It is a long journey and she hardly ever visits because of the distance. But she always comes on my birthday.

You are my only niece, May Amelia, and that is cause for celebration any day, Aunt Alice always says.

Aunt Alice is Mamma's sister from Boston and hasn't got a husband but still she looks just fine to me. I may not have a husband if I can live like Aunt Alice in her lovely house in Astoria. Wilbert says that it has a flower garden in the back and real photographs of folks on the walls and always smells like a lady, not like a cow.

Mamma looks real tired when we come in; her dark hair is drooping out of the bun and her shoulders are sagging. She is rubbing the place on her belly where the new baby is growing. Mamma takes one look at Wilbert and me and Bosie standing there dripping wet and says, I sure hope you children caught some fish if you took a dunk in the Nasel.

Yeah, says Kaarlo nastily. You were gone long enough. Sure you weren't up at Ben Armstrong's camp May Amelia? he says, trying to get me into trouble.

Shut up Kaarlo, I say.

Don't be mean to May, Wendell says, it's her birthday. Wendell is such a good brother; he is always sticking up for me.

What did you catch May? Matti asks gently.

Did you catch salmon? Ivan and Alvin say together.

Hush boys, Mamma says. Did you catch any fish at all, May?

I shrug.

No, Wilbert says with a grin, but we caught a dog.

Aunt Alice shoos Wilbert and all the boys out of the kitchen and says, May, why don't you and I fix supper and let your poor sweet mamma rest awhile before she drops that babe of hers right here on the rug?

10

Aunt Alice is wearing a fine rose-colored silk dress with real shell buttons and her hair is shiny and golden and tied up in a fancy bob with ribbons. I don't think I've ever seen Mamma in a dress as pretty as Aunt Alice's. She most often wears a black cotton skirt and a white blouse. And since Aunt Alice looks so pretty and Mamma is sitting down drinking the cider that Alice has brought, I go about fixing supper real quiet-like so that they can talk and tell secrets. Aunt Alice treats me as if I am all grown up and not only twelve, which is fine by me because I mostly feel as if I am practically a hundred years old.

Aunt Alice says to Mamma, Dear Alma, why you've had some child in that stomach of yours forever it seems, haven't you had enough? I thought you weren't going to have any more.

Mamma just sits there and says, Alice are you here to help or to hinder 'cause I ain't abiding any hinderers right now.

I'm a helper Mamma, I say.

You sure are darling. Thank God for May. Alice, I swear all these boys put together wouldn't know how to butter a slice of bread if there wasn't a woman in the room.

That's just their nature Alma, says Alice smoothing down her fine skirt. After seven boys I would've thought you'd be used to them by now.

I hope you have a girl Mamma, I say. We can call her Little Alice after Aunt Alice.

Aunt Alice smiles at me. Why May Amelia you really are a dear, she says. Who would've thought there would be such a lady way out here in the middle of nowhere?

Nasel is truly in the middle of nowhere—why, there's nothing here but land and trees and elk and sheep and bears and boys. Mostly boys though. There haven't been any girls born out here since me and I am the only young girl in the Island Schoolhouse. Sometimes I see Chinook Indian girls when I am in the woods but the closest Finnish girls my age are near Knappton, too far for playing.

The front door opens and Uncle Henry and Aunt Feenie come in carrying a box with a yellow bow. Aunt Feenie is Pappa's sister and she is married to Uncle Henry and they are my favorite relations after Aunt Alice because they are so nice to Wilbert and me. Uncle Henry is much older than Aunt Feenie and Pappa says Feenie married him for his riches although I cannot imagine what Pappa means because they have no more money than us and we do not have hardly any at all.

12

Mamma says Pappa is a stubborn old Finn who doesn't like foreigners and not to mind him.

Uncle Henry is Scottish, not Finnish like everybody else around here, but I don't think it matters one bit because he is the smartest person I have ever met. Why, he can speak five languages on account of being a famous sea captain. His real name is Neal McNeil and Mamma says that he changed his name when he came to America because of some trouble he had back in Scotland. Now he is just Henry Smith, which is very American indeed. He has a room in his house filled with nothing but books. We don't have enough books to fill even one shelf. Pappa says they have a room for books because they could not have a baby on account of Uncle Henry always being away at sea.

Well, if it isn't my favorite niece! Uncle Henry says with a smile, swooping me into his arms for a bear hug. He even looks like a bear, with his bushy red beard and broad chest and big belly.

I am all sticky and my braid has come undone and my shirt has got mud on it from the dunking in the Nasel. I do not look like a birthday girl, and in Wilbert's old torn dungarees I don't think I look much like a girl at all. Uncle Henry eyes me and shakes his head.

13

May Amelia, you look like you've been shang-haied! Uncle Henry roars with a laugh.

Aunt Feenie hands me the box. This is for you, May. Happy birthday dear.

Uncle Henry wanders off to the porch where Pappa is smoking his pipe and I tear open the box.

It is a baby doll. She is the most beautiful baby doll I have ever seen with a real china face and a white silk dress. Truly, it is the loveliest thing I have ever owned.

Do you like her May? Aunt Feenie asks anx-iously. Aunt Feenie is not as pretty as Aunt Alice, but she has a kind heart. Her eyes are gray as a gull's wing and have a sad pull to them. I think she wishes she had a child.

It's a fine doll, Mamma says.

Wilbert, Wendell, Ivan, Alvin, Kaarlo, and Isaiah crowd around me.

It sure is pretty May Amelia, Wendell says. I reckon I could help you make another dress for it.

What're you gonna call her May? Wilbert says.

Baby Feenie, I say, looking at my aunt.

Aunt Feenie smiles.

A minute later my big brother Matti comes in carting a wooden crate. He sets it down in front of me with a grunt.

14

It's from all us boys, May Amelia, Matti says. Happy birthday.

I take the lid off the crate and inside is a fine, sturdy-looking carved wooden pirate ship attached to a long string.

It's for Susannah, Alvin says. Susannah is my rag doll.

So that she can search for treasure, Isaiah suggests.

And go out on the Nasel, Ivan says.

Even when you can't May Amelia! Wilbert says, and everybody laughs, even Kaarlo.

Wilbert and I go out to the porch where Uncle Henry is sitting with Pappa. Uncle Henry is a famous sea captain and has traveled everywhere. Why, he has been to the Sandwich Islands and the East Indies even. He always has stories about sailors being shanghaied all the way to the Orient. He says they fall asleep in their beds and wake up on a bunk in the rolling waves. You can take me to China anytime, I always tell Uncle Henry. I'd do anything to get away from Nasel. I'd be happy to get shanghaied, even if I did wake up on the China Sea.

Uncle Henry leans forward and puffs on his ivory pipe.

15

I was just telling your father here about the time I sailed around Cape Horn up to San Francisco and toward the Shoalwater Bay. I very nearly didn't make it that time. When we reached Cape Disappointment, our ship got caught in an awful storm and nearly crashed into the cliff rocks, he says.

I guess that's why the old sailors call it Cape Disappointment Uncle Henry, I say.

He says, I guess so Miss May Amelia, and wasn't I nearly the fool to pay no mind to the salty old dogs?

At supper Mamma tells us children that Aunt Feenie is going to stay with us for a spell on account of Uncle Henry's sailing trip.

Where are you off to now Henry? Aunt Alice asks.

Heading to San Francisco, Alice, Uncle Henry says between bites. Fine stew you got here Alma.

Aunt Feenie says she'll be right lonely with Henry being gone and has decided to get a cooking job with Nora Fuller at Ben Armstrong's logging camp which is situated a few miles away up the Nasel from our farm. The forest heading up to Ben Armstrong's is too thick for roads so the loggers use the Nasel to get the logs down. We live at the bay of the Nasel, and that's where all the logs from Armstong's logging camp eventually float down to.

We'll be happy to have you here Feenie, won't we May Amelia? Mamma says with a wink at me. The boys will sort you out a bed.

I am so excited I can hardly contain my own self just imagining Aunt Feenie living with us! It will only be until Uncle Henry gets back from sea she tells me but I say *fine*, fine, that's plenty long. It's almost as nice a gift as the baby doll.

When everyone is in bed I whisper to Wilbert. Wilbert and I share a room at the back of the house, near the barn, and sometimes I can hear the cows lowing.

I wish we could live with Uncle Henry and Aunt Feenie in Astoria, I say.

We can't May, Wilbert whispers back.

How come?

Because we just can't, he says. We have to help mind the farm.

I know this too but I wish we didn't have to always Mind The Farm. I am busy with chores and whatnot nearly all the time now since Mamma has got the baby coming, there is hardly ever any time

17

for tricks and adventures these days. We are up at the crack of dawn and in bed later and later every night.

The door creaks open and Wendell creeps in and sets on our bed. Wendell is my second-favorite brother after Wilbert. Wendell wears eyeglasses on account of being blind as a bat and he squints at us in the candlelight. Pappa had to go all the way to Astoria to fetch the glasses for him.

Kaarlo's snoring is too loud, he says, I won't get a wink. I'm sleeping in here. Shove on over Wilbert.

Wilbert moves over and now there are three children in a bed meant for two.

I've been telling Wilbert here that I want to leave the farm, I say.

I want to leave the farm too, May Amelia. I'll never learn to be a doctor in these parts, Wendell says.

Wendell has always wanted to be a real doctor and I suspect one day he will if he ever gets off the farm. Wendell is always saying that I can do whatever I want to do, that the best thing for me would be to get off the farm and go out into the wide world. He always tells me that I have *sisu*, which is Finnish for guts, and that I can do anything. It

18

always makes me feel better when he tells me this.

Outside the window the sky is black and the stars are winking at me. I watch the fireflies dancing in the field and realize my birthday is nearly over, and I haven't made my secret birthday wish yet. Mamma says that a wish made on a birthday always comes true. I don't know about that, though. Last year I wished for Kaarlo to stop being so mean to me all the time but he's still the same mean old Kaarlo.

Still, it can't hurt to try. I think hard but it's an easy wish. I can't tell anyone, not even Wilbert and he is my very best brother. I can't tell him because he'll never understand what it is like to be me, May Amelia Jackson, the only Jackson girl, and the only girl in Nasel.

I squeeze my eyes tight and wish hard with my heart that Mamma has a little baby girl so that I can have a sister.

I just made my birthday wish, I whisper. But Wilbert and Wendell aren't listening to me.

They're too busy snoring.

CHAPTER TWO

There Ain't No Gentlemen on the Nasel

When Auntie Alice leaves in the morning she asks Mamma if the twins, Ivan and Alvin, can go to Astoria to help mend her roof. We are in the kitchen discussing this when Alvin and Ivan come banging down the stairs. Their hair is all mussed up from sleeping funny, and it's sticking straight up in places. The twins squint sleepily at us.

It'll be nice to have gentlemen around, Aunt Alice says, skeptically eyeing the twins.

Mamma just sighs.

Since Aunt Alice has no man of her own she has to borrow my brothers which is just fine by me. I do not mind one bit lending them out from time to time.

I'll send them along to you tomorrow, Mamma says. May, you and Wilbert can go too. I need you to shop for me while the boys tend to Alice's roof. We need just about everything.

I can barely stand the whole rest of the day. I can't wait to go to Astoria, and for the whole weekend! I have never been to Astoria and have only heard about it from the boys. Pappa always says it is Too Rough And Wild for a young girl like me.

Aunt Feenie comes down and I tell her the good news.

I am going to Astoria, I say.

Good for you May. I'll look after your mamma while you are gone. I know how much work you've been doing around here lately but I'm here now and I'll lend a hand when I can.

I am the first one up in the morning and finish my chores quick as can be. Pappa comes down the stairs and says suspiciously, What are you doing up so early May Amelia? He knows I am not fond of getting up early.

Pappa always calls me May Amelia when I am in trouble.

We're going to Astoria, I say.

Pappa frowns and says, I don't know if that's such a good idea.

Mamma walks in and pats Pappa on the shoulder

and says, I need May to do some shopping for me. It's too far for me to travel with the baby on the way and I can't spare anyone else right now. Let her go, Jalmer. The boys'll keep an eye on her.

Pappa just looks at me long and hard, so hard his shaggy eyebrows meet, and finally he says You Best Not Get Into Mischief! and stomps out of the kitchen.

Mamma says Be Careful Children; May Amelia Be Sure To Mind Your Brothers and be back by supper on Sunday.

Out here in Washington there are no roads but we have the Nasel. We use the Nasel to go everywhere, even to school. It is the only way to get around. I learnt how to navigate on the Nasel when I was only five, Wilbert taught me, and I think I'm good but Wilbert's the only one of the boys who will let me steer the boat.

Our schoolhouse is on the Smith Island which is in the middle of the Nasel. We are close enough to the Pacific Ocean that sometimes we cannot go to school if the tides are not with us. You also have to be careful of all the snags in the water, what with the logging men sending lumber downriver. Sometimes they pile up like beaver houses and the boat gets stuck.

Me and Wilbert and Alvin and Ivan must go to Knappton, where we will catch the boat to Astoria. We can take the little rowboat partways, but then we will have to tie it up and walk the rest of the way to Knappton, which is quite far indeed. One time Pappa had his tonsils taken out by a doctor in Astoria at the St. Mary's Hospital with no ether or anything and then he took the boat from Astoria to Knappton and then ran all the way back home! After the boys heard that story, Alvin and Ivan ran the whole way from Knappton to our house, never once stopping only just to prove that they were as strong as Pappa. I am sure I could run that far myself, even though Kaarlo says that girls can't run for spit. But he forgets that I can spit right well.

The sunny sun is out a-shining which it hardly ever does and the Nasel is as calm and smooth as the inside of a clam shell. We pass by the Petersen farm and our friend Lonny Petersen waves to us and runs down to the side of the water. The Petersens are the only Finnish family on this part of the Nasel that have a savusauna, a smoke sauna, and so folks are always dropping by to enjoy it.

Pappa helped Mr. Petersen build the sauna, which resembles a small cabin. They used cedar wood so it smells real fine and it sets right on the Nasel so a body can have a dip when it gets too hot from the rock furnace which it most often does. All the Finns love the sauna, including me, especially in the winter. We undress down to our drawers and sit in the hot sauna till our bones feel like they're melting. Then when it gets too hot we run out and jump right into the Nasel and cool off till our skin tingles all over. It's heaps more fun than taking a bath and you get just as clean. Mamma says that back in Finland the doctors wouldn't see a body unless they'd been in the sauna first.

Hi Lonny, I say.

Where ya going May? Lonny says. Lonny is a little slow, and has trouble understanding things. He has a terrible hard time speaking English in school. Me and Lonny always speak in Finnish when we are not in school even though Mamma says I am not helping him one bit.

We're going to Astoria to see my Aunt Alice.

Can I come?

No Lonny, I say. Not this time.

He shakes his head sadly. Lonny is a big boy, wide and strong, but his mind is like a small boy's on account of an accident he had when he was

25

small. You have to explain everything to him.

How come? he says.

Just because Lonny. We'll see you when we come home, I call.

'Bye May, 'bye Wilbert, 'bye Alvin, 'bye Ivan, he yells, waving.

And as we turn the bend in the Nasel, Lonny is still there, waving to us from the shore.

Alvin and Ivan are rowing the boat and Wilbert is cleaning his gun. These brothers of mine are always cleaning their guns, you would think we were in the middle of a war right now. They are always talking about wars and Confederates and Unionmen and such. They go and hear stories from Jacob Clayton on the next farm over, who fought on the Southern side and lost three fingers on his left hand. He has only his thumb and fore-finger, and when he points it looks as if his hand is a small gun; that is the shape it makes.

Mr. Clayton is always telling my brothers about the battles, and the ambushes, and all the men he saw killed. He talks about having the dysentery all through one winter, no shoes to speak of, nothing to eat but dried-out rotting venison and how he deserted the army after he got his fingers shot off by a boy of no more than twelve. He says he had to crawl over piles of dead bodies to get off the battlefield and that when he got off he passed out from the pain and woke up in a farmhouse with all the other wounded and a surgeon was going to saw off his hand. When he saw the surgeon with the sawblade he pulled out his knife and put it to the surgeon's throat and told him that he'd gut the man sooner than let him cut off his hand. After that he ran away, joined up with a group of home-steaders who were heading west. And now he is our closest neighbor two miles over on the Nasel.

I am always amazed that he traded all that excitement just to be a farmer.

The barrel of Wilbert's gun is glinting in the sun and I say, Let me see your gun here Wilbert.

Wilbert hands me his gun and I look down the long barrel.

I want to learn how to shoot, I say.

Alvin and Ivan look at each other at the same time and Ivan shakes his shiny blond head. All my brothers have fine blond Finnish hair except Wilbert whose hair is white. When Wilbert goes hunting with Wild Cat Clark he puts mud on his hair so that he blends in with the pine trees which I think is a very good idea. Me, I don't have any

27

Finnish blond hair; mine's brown as the bottom of the Nasel. I don't think Pappa likes me because I haven't got blond hair like the rest of the boys. Mamma says that I stand out like a brown elk in a blond herd. It makes me lonely sometimes, being the only one that's different. It makes me wish even harder for a little sister.

Pappa'll kill us for sure if we let you shoot that gun, Alvin says. Shotgun shells are very expensive indeed. They are so expensive that when the boys go hunting Pappa tells them that if they do not kill two geese with every shot then we are losing money.

But what if I'm by myself and a cougar attacks me or a bear even? I say. There are black bears everywhere and they are very fierce. Kaarlo and Matti got chased nearly all the way home by a bear one time. Why, the bend in the Nasel by Jacob Clayton's farm is called Bear Bend on account of the bears always fishing there. Mamma always says No Swimming At Bear Bend.

Wilbert is on my side. Yeah, May ought to know how to shoot, he says.

She's a girl, Alvin and Ivan say together.

But she's twelve now! Wilbert says, exasperated.

Alvin and Ivan exchange a look. Sometimes I

wonder if they read each other's thoughts because they are twins. Mamma says that when Alvin and Ivan were born it was like a miracle. Imagine having two whole babes where there was only supposed to be one.

Well? I say. Can I?

They both nod reluctantly.

I want to learn right now! I say, excited.

But Aunt Alice is expecting us this afternoon, Ivan says.

Alvin and Ivan seem like they're always minding everybody, 'cause they never get into trouble like me. But Wilbert tells me that they are really mischievous and that they never get into trouble on account of being so sneaky and sly.

She won't mind if we're a little late, I say. We'll be there all weekend.

We are not far from Olaaf Kuula's farm.

Let's tie the boat up over by that stone, Wilbert says.

Alvin and Ivan paddle us to shore.

Is it safe to stop here? Alvin says.

Everybody knows that Olaaf Kuula has been crazy ever since the Nasel flooded his farmland. It's now mostly marshy tidelands, but Olaaf Kuula won't leave and he survives by boarding local gillnetters. Olaaf Kuula claims that his land is haunted by ghosts that followed him over from Jyväskylä, Finland. Pappa says Olaaf Kuula has been in the bottle ever since the flood and sees strange things on account of it.

Sure, Wilbert says, not sounding very sure at all.

We walk a little bit into the tidelands where no one is likely to see us. Alvin ties a cattail around a tree with the brown furry piece in the front. You're gonna aim at this right here, Alvin says, waving the cat.

Wilbert puts his gun in my arms and shows me how to hold it. It's big and nearly as heavy as Bosie.

When you fire it's gonna hit your shoulder, Wilbert says. You have to look down the barrel to aim.

I take a deep breath and hold the gun. It is my only chance. I just know if I miss the boys won't let me try again. And I know I am just as good as any boy. Wilbert is staring at me hard, a stare that says You Can Do It. Time's a-wasting. I pull the trigger and the gun explodes. It jerks out of my arm and fires into the air and I land flat on my back.

Are you all right May? Wilbert says.

Did I miss? I ask.

All of a sudden there is a gunshot in the marsh and a flock of ducks goes flying into the sky. A wild-looking man appears riding an old shaggy mare. The mare and the man resemble each other, they are both so scruffy-looking. The man is waving a rifle in the air and shaking his fist at us.

It's Olaaf Kuula!

Where's Alvin and Ivan? I say, looking around, but they are nowhere to be seen.

Come on May, Wilbert says, pulling at me. Hurry!

Olaaf Kuula is riding fast toward us on his mare.

You ghosts get out of here before I tan your backsides! he hollers, taking aim at us.

We ain't ghosts! I shout but Wilbert grabs my arm and says, He's Crazy May Run!

But Olaaf Kuula's gaining on us and he fires a shot, just missing.

Faster May! Wilbert shouts.

All of a sudden Alvin pops up in the middle of the marsh.

You crazy old man! Alvin yells.

Olaaf Kuula whirls around and takes a shot at Alvin.

Alvin ducks down quick as can be.

I hear him moan like he is shot.

Got ya good, you trespassing ghost. That'll teach ya! Olaaf Kuula yells shakily.

Alvin's shot! I say.

He's faking, says Wilbert. Let's go.

Olaaf Kuula turns his attention back on us, and we duck down into the grass.

Just then, on the other side of the marsh, Ivan pops his head up. He is the exact picture of Alvin.

You crazy old man! Ivan hollers, repeating Alvin's words like he is a ghost.

Olaaf Kuula looks at Ivan, and then back over to where he fired at Alvin.

I just shot you! Olaaf Kuula says, confused now. You're haunting me, you ghosts!

Alvin pops up and the twins say in unison, We surely are.

And we'll keep on haunting you as long as you keep shooting at us! Alvin shouts.

Get offa my farm, Olaaf Kuula moans, sounding scared.

He really thinks they're ghosts, I say.

He's drunk as a skunk May, Wilbert says.

Olaaf Kuula peers at Alvin and Ivan and moans some more.

32

Hurry! Wilbert calls to Ivan and Alvin, and they run quickly toward us.

We jump into the rowboat and start rowing as fast as we can. Olaaf Kuula rides his horse along the bank. He takes aim and fires at us. We all duck down. The shot clips our boat and splinters go flying.

Stay offa my farm, you blasted ghosts! Go back to Jyväskylä, he hollers, shaking his fist.

The fast-moving Nasel rescues us and when we look back he is just a speck on the shore.

Wilbert eyes the spot where Olaaf Kuula got the boat. Pappa's gonna kill us, he says with certainty.

That's the truth for sure.

By the time we reach Astoria nearly four hours later after the long walk and then the boat ride, we are exhausted for sure. But as we pull into the harbor my eyes widen at the very sight of this town. It is like nothing I have ever seen.

This is Astoria: a seamen's village with houses perched on the cliffs overlooking the bay like eggs on hay, waiting to teeter off. The houses are fancy, nothing at all like the farmhouses of Nasel. Astorian houses have scallops of gingerbread trim around all the porches and roofs and doors and some of them are painted so pretty that they look just like cakes waiting to be eaten by a hungry giant. The docks are crowded with boats and sailors and Chinooks and gillnetters, the salmon fishermen. Gillnetters have their own special boat called a bateau which has sails that look like the delicate wings of a bat. Uncle Henry says that the bateaux resemble boats from China called junks and that sometimes when he looks down at the bay crowded with bateaux he thinks he is back in the Orient.

Pappa says that Astoria is a wild roughneck town full of lawless roughriders and swindlers and harlots but it looks pretty tame to me. In the teeming crowds I notice strange-looking men with slender eyes and long black pigtails. They are all wearing loose-fitting trousers and long tops that resemble nightshirts. They aren't Chinooks but what could they be?

Wilbert catches me eyeing the strange-looking men and says, Why, they're Chinamen May. Haven't you ever seen a Chinaman?

No Wilbert, I say, exasperated, I've never been out of Nasel—how do you expect I would ever have seen a real live Chinaman?

I have heard of the Orient and the Chinamen

from Uncle Henry, but this is the first time I have seen one in person.

Whew, Wilbert says, crinkling his nose. It's stinkier than a cow stall.

And he's right. Between all the smells of fresh fish and ripe sailors it's pretty smelly down near the docks. There is a salmon cannery setting right on the docks and it appears that they are just throwing all the fish guts right back into the water, and that is no doubt the cause of the fierce smell.

As we make our way up the winding road to Aunt Alice's house at the top of the hill, the salty ocean air breezes across my face. It is quite a climb to where Aunt Alice lives and it is getting dark.

Wilbert tugs on my arm and says, Look around there will you May?

I turn around and see the most glorious sunset on the bay, it is as if the very sun is sinking into the water, bleeding every color pink as it goes down.

Red at night, seaman's delight; bloody in the morning, sailor takes warning, Ivan says. That's what Uncle Henry always says.

I wonder when Uncle Henry will be back from his voyages.

Soon I imagine, May Amelia, says Alvin. He was

only going to San Francisco, not very far at all.

When we reach Aunt Alice's house, she is sitting on her pretty porch on a rocking chair with a glass of something in her hand. Wilbert says it is wine.

She is so very beautiful, my aunt, with her shiny bright hair twisted high on her head like a lady, not like Mamma with her knot all falling apart. She is wearing a dress the color of a robin's egg and from the way it shines I know it is silk and there are tiny polished buttons from the top to the bottom. She looks like a real live princess.

I was worried about you gentlemen, Aunt Alice says. Did you have a late start?

Wilbert says, Well you see—

Ivan cuts Wilbert off and says, Pappa wanted us to help him bring in the sheeps and they were in an ornery mood.

I can see what Wilbert means about Ivan and Alvin being so sneaky. It is not a bad lie.

Yeah, Alvin says, we had to dig 'em out of the muck in the swamp.

Oh my, she says. It sounds like a real adventure.

Alvin, Ivan, and Wilbert roll their eyes and give me a look that says only Aunt Alice would think that sheep mucking is an adventure.

May, what a cunning little dress that is on your

36

doll. Did your mamma make that for you? Aunt Alice says.

Wendell made it, I say. With gunnysack.

Wendell made it? Well that's not something you hear about gentlemen doing every day, she says, arching her eyebrow.

I have been practicing my sewing and mending on Susannah, my doll. She is a rag doll with a cotton face and button eyes, not fancy like the baby doll Aunt Feenie gave me. I don't play with the baby doll for fear of it breaking.

My brother Wendell who is very clever at mending and sewing things has been teaching me how to draw dress patterns and stitch them up. He even made Susannah some hair out of yarn he had saved. So now Wendell and I are making Susannah a whole new wardrobe out of gunnysack and flour sack. I tell him that he will be a very good doctor indeed if he can sew up folks half as good as he sews for Susannah. She is a lucky doll.

Well, Aunt Alice says, I am simply thrilled that you are at my humble house, so please dears, do come inside and let's retire to the dining room. I've prepared all your favorites. Baked salmon, clam chowder, Yorkshire pudding, and roasted potatoes, I believe, she says, ticking off her fingers.

37

I look at the table she has spread out and say, All Of This is for us children? There is so much food I cannot remember when I ever did see so much food. It has been a bad year on the farm on account of two of our milking cows getting stuck in the tidelands and dying.

She says, Of course May Amelia, go on child, eat, before you faint from hunger. You could use some meat on your bones.

It is a feast. I eat and eat. There is so much food, I eat almost as much as Wilbert and Ivan and Alvin, but they eat more because they are boys and have much bigger stomachs. The food is not like what we usually have at the farm. At home we most often have Finnish dishes. Why, even the gravy Aunt Alice serves with the salmon is made with real cream and it is white and delicious, not all gristly-looking like what I am used to, especially when I am doing the cooking.

This is nice food, I say.

I'm glad you like it dear. It's English food.

Aunt Alice has not kept to the Finnish ways. She almost always speaks English and now she is cooking English food. She is good at being American.

After supper we sit on the front porch looking

down at the whole town of Astoria sparkling below. There is a bright full moon, and the boats in the harbor are lit up and dancing in the inky water. Aunt Alice gives us big bowls of blackberries with fresh-whipped cream for dessert. Both Ivan and Alvin love fresh cream. They gulp theirs down fast.

Can I have some more? Ivan says.

Me too, Alvin says.

And me, says Wilbert.

I want some too, I say, holding out my bowl.

Aunt Alice shakes her head and says, I don't know how much cream is left.

Well I asked first, Ivan says.

I want some too, I say. You're such a hog Ivan.

Children, behave, Aunt Alice says. Ivan and Alvin, why don't you go into the kitchen and make up bowls for everyone?

Ivan and Alvin gather up our bowls and disappear into the kitchen. They come back with big bowls of berries with cream on top. Ivan gives me the bowl with the most cream. Aunt Alice smiles approvingly.

Well done, Ivan. A gentleman always looks after the ladies.

See, I'm not the hog this time May Amelia, he says.

39

Thank you kindly, I say.

What nice manners you have, May Amelia, Aunt Alice says.

All of a sudden there is a huge noise from far below on the docks. It is the sound of a dozen guns firing, and there are sparks throwing off light. I can hear laughter and clapping.

What's going on? Wilbert says, leaping up to look down below at the commotion.

That's the Chinamen and their firecrackers, Aunt Alice says. They must be celebrating something. Lord knows they have little enough to celebrate.

What are firecrackers? I say.

They're these things that crackle and pop. All the Chinamen love firecrackers. They're very festive. Kind of like a shivaree.

A Finnish shivaree is when a bunch of folks get together and bang pots and pans and make a lot of noise to celebrate. They usually do shivarees at weddings and birthdays.

I want to get me some of those firecrackers, I think.

I sure do miss living back east, in Boston. It was such a fine place to live. Aunt Alice sighs, staring into the fire.

40

I look around her porch and think of her fancy house and it seems pretty fine to me. Why, there are real crystal lamps and woven rugs from India and everything a body could want.

Aunt Alice, I say, how come you got so much money and no husband?

Aunt Alice just laughs and says, You are such a dear thing, May Amelia. I have a gentleman friend and he provides me with money and such.

Wilbert gives me a wink. I wonder why.

I take a big bite of my blackberries and cream. My face scrunches all up and Ivan and Alvin start laughing. They didn't put cream on my berries— they put the leftover cream gravy from dinner!

Is something wrong with the berries, May? Aunt Alice says.

I shake my head. Mamma always says Mind Your Manners.

Alvin whispers into Wilbert's ear and he starts laughing too at my predicament.

I fix all the boys with a look.

Why I would sure like one of them gentleman friends, Aunt Alice, I say. There ain't no gentlemen on the Nasel. Just a bunch of no-good brothers.

That's the truth for sure.

41

CHAPTER THREE

∽◦⌒

There Are Miracles
and There Are Sheeps

The preacher's sermon today was all about miracles.

I usually sleep during the sermon on account of it being so boring but this time I paid attention as everyone is always telling me that I Am A Miracle. I suspect that there are other sorts of miracles besides no-good girls.

After the service, Wilbert and me and Ivan and Alvin and Matti are walking and I say, It certainly was a miracle that Pappa didn't tan our hides for getting the boat all shot up.

Alvin says, Yes indeed it was a miracle.

Ivan says, Yep, it was a miracle.

Wilbert says, That's for sure.

Matti laughs at us and says, It will be a Real Miracle if you can manage to stay out of trouble for more than a day May Amelia.

When we get back to the farm, Pappa has a stern look on his face.

I want all you children to tend to the sheep today, he says. Round 'em up, count 'em, and mend 'em.

But Pappa, I say. Me and Wilbert were set on going to the Baby Island and fishing. It's Sunday.

May, I'm only telling you once. I want you to go out with your brother Isaiah and help him with the sheep. The fish will still be there another day, Pappa says with a scowl.

Tending to the sheeps. A more trying thing I cannot think of doing because all about our land are hedges and hedges of evergreen blackberry vines with prickly thorns. The sheeps get stuck on the thorns and mew like cats until they rip themselves free and then they are hurt real bad. There is wool all over the blackberry bushes.

Isaiah says that it looks as if the Jackson family is raising wool bushes, not sheeps.

My brother Isaiah loves the sheeps better than us children, I sometimes think. It is his job to mind them most of the time and Mamma calls him her Patient Shepherd. Isaiah has a soft voice and gentle touch and the sheeps don't startle when he is near. He spends so much time tending to the sheeps that he most often smells like one. Isaiah's blond hair has a curl to it and Wilbert says it looks woolly like the sheeps.

Isaiah says the sheeps look more like people than animals and he gives them names after all our neighbors. There's Jacob Clayton who lives across the way and has a long face; there's the Widow Katja Krohn who always has a sad look about her; and there's Mrs. Petersen, Lonny's ma, who lives out by the south field across the swamp.

Maybe Isaiah is a little crazy naming all the sheeps after folks, but sometimes I think he has a point. Wilbert tells me they are practically as stupid as people, the way they are always getting tangled up in the blackberry brambles.

Me and Wilbert and Ivan and Alvin and Kaarlo and Wendell and Isaiah walk out to the back pasture where the sheeps are grazing. Isaiah has built all the fences around the pasture where the sheeps graze and they are fine fences—they never fall apart like other folks'. Isaiah is the best builder of the boys, always on hand to do something. Besides tending sheeps, Isaiah loves carpentering. He made my dresser and the stand in the kitchen. He is so good with wood and all that

I suspect he will someday make his mark with wooden things.

Kaarlo grouses. Those sheeps were a lousy investment, he says. Old Mr. Krouer tricked your pa into buying them.

Kaarlo is almost always in a bad mood and there is nothing he hates more than tending to the sheeps.

Isaiah looks hurt. You're wrong, Kaarlo. The sheeps are good, he says.

Kaarlo laughs but not in a nice way. He thinks Isaiah has spent so much time with the sheeps that he thinks like one.

Good? The wool's no good 'cause it ends up on the darn bushes, and they ain't even good-tasting animals.

Isaiah goes all pale. He hates it more than anything when Pappa has to slaughter a sheep. He never eats mutton when I cook it for supper. He says he'd rather starve.

Hush Up Kaarlo, Wilbert says, eyeing Isaiah, the sheeps are no trouble at all.

I think Wilbert should be a judge or lawman when he is big, the way he is always trying to keep the peace between us children.

We spend all day rounding up the twenty-nine

46

sheeps and checking to see if they've cut themselves on the brambles and it's no fun for sure. It's hot as can be now that it is July and the sheeps are in a real ornery mood.

One of the sheeps has got some bad cuts and Ivan and Alvin must slather some flaxseed poultice on it so it doesn't get infected. But this sheep is cranky and bad-tempered, and when Alvin tries to slather on the medicine it takes a bite of his hand.

Dumb sheep! Alvin says with a grimace, shaking his hand. It got me good.

Ivan swats the sheep's back end and hollers, Bad Sheep! No Biting!

Isaiah goes running over and hollers, Don't Yell At The Sheeps!

There he goes, Kaarlo says rolling his eyes, acting all crazy.

The sheeps smell real bad, worse than horses and cows put together. I remember the sermon.

Boy, these sheeps sure aren't miracles, I say.

It'll be a miracle if we finish tending to them before bedtime, Kaarlo mutters.

I smell like a sheep, I say.

You smell fine to me May, Isaiah says.

He would say that, seeing as he smells like a sheep himself.

47

You're the smelliest girl in Nasel, Wilbert teases.
I'm the *only* girl in Nasel, I say.
And that's the truth for sure.

After we have finished and are washing up for supper Isaiah comes running home. Jacob Clayton is by and is helping Pappa mend the barn.

Isaiah opens the door and yells, Hurry! Mrs. Petersen has broken her back out in the south field.

He runs back off toward the field and Mr. Clayton and Pappa drop what they are doing and Pappa says, Go On Wilbert, go fetch Lonny and tell him to head out to the field—his ma's hurt.

So Wilbert takes off and Mr. Clayton and Pappa and I run out to the south field, and sure enough we see Lonny Petersen and Wilbert running toward us and there is Isaiah in the middle of the field, in the tall grass, waving his arms.

We get there and Isaiah is petting a sheep lying on its side.

Pappa's out of breath and Mr. Clayton too. Lonny says, Where's My Ma, Isaiah?

Isaiah looks up at us and starts to blush.

Pappa's looking around now and says, Yes, Isaiah, where is Mrs. Petersen at?

She's lying right here Pa.

You mean that sheep lying there?

Yeah Pa. That's what I call this here sheep and her back is surely broken.

Wilbert starts laughing and laughing and soon enough we are all laughing, even Pappa. Pappa laughing is a sight indeed, because his white eyebrows scrunch up. Pappa hardly ever laughs.

Isaiah, we thought you meant Mrs. Petersen, Lonny's ma, I say.

Yeah, says Lonny. I'm sure glad it ain't but you are right Isaiah that sheep does bear a resemblance to my ma, but don't tell her I said so.

Pappa had to shoot Mrs. Petersen the sheep 'cause we could do nothing for her and I suspect we will be having mutton stew for supper.

I am the one who ended up cooking Mrs. Petersen for supper.

Aunt Feenie is most often late for dinner on account of her having to feed all the men at the logging camp. I thought she would be around the house more, but she is gone before I get up in the morning and real tired by the time she gets home at night. She says it is a lot of work to cook for twenty-five men. I am still knee deep in chores, at least until Mamma has the baby.

There've been a lot of accidents lately at the camp, Aunt Feenie says at supper.

I notice that Isaiah is having none of the mutton stew, only vegetables. Every few minutes he gives me a hurt look, a look that says, How Can You Eat Mrs. Petersen?

Like what? Pappa asks.

Aunt Feenie lowers her voice like she is telling a secret.

Well, she says in a confiding tone, all the logging men have been saying that the woods are cursed by the Indians, there being strange accidents and all. Anja Printh's son Oscar had a tree fall on his leg today and was hurt real bad and it gave all the men a chill. They had to take him upriver to Dr. Gray and he might lose his leg.

Everyone at the table gasps.

I cannot think of a worse thing. Dr. Gray is not even a real doctor but there isn't anybody else who knows medicine in these parts and the nearest real doctor is all the way down in Astoria.

But Dr. Gray just peddles fake tonics and pretends at being a doctor, Wendell says.

Wendell's right, Mamma says. I wouldn't send Bosie to Dr. Gray. He's got no learning and all he sells to sick folks is hope.

They're Indian woods, Pappa says. I warned Ben Armstrong when he told me he intended to

set up that logging camp and so did Jacob
Clayton. We've been here a lot longer than young
Ben and know this area a sound sight better than
him, all green like he is coming from New York. I
have a bad feeling about those woods where Ben's
a-logging.

Matti says, They're sure for certain burial
woods.

Pappa grunts and nods his head in agreement.
Pappa respects Matti because he is so responsible
and because he is the oldest.

Wilbert says, Pappa I've seen the Indians burying on the Baby Island.

Pappa shakes his head like a cranky bear.

That may be but Ben Armstrong's woods are
where the Indians used to bury the dead ones
before we got here. There's bad blood in the very
ground, guarantee my words, I once found an elk
all gutted up no heart there at all or eyes either
and its blood was drawn all over the trees. No
wolf or bear can paint blood on trees. You children stay away from those woods.

The stars are so high in the sky that I imagine
the angels themselves are holding them up and
that this must be a miracle.

There is a big owl hooting right outside our window. The Chinooks say that when an owl hoots it means that some spirit is wandering and I suspect that they are right but I sure do wish this owl would stop hooting so we could sleep.

Wilbert, I say, I wonder if our sheeps are safe out in the pasture when a cursed Indian spirit is wandering around?

Oh May, Wilbert says. Our sheeps smell so nasty that if I was a cursed Indian spirit I wouldn't go near them.

Then we're safe too, I say, taking a whiff of my own sheep-smelling self.

Wilbert laughs.

At least until we get our bath, he says.

Isaiah tells me that because I was such a help with the sheeps he will take me fishing on the Baby Island.

I'd rather go with you Wilbert, I say.

You hafta go May, Wilbert says. It's not every day that Isaiah prefers your company to the sheeps.

Wilbert speaks the truth. Isaiah's still not talking to Ivan and Alvin on account of Ivan hollering at the sick sheep.

We row out to the Baby Island and Isaiah takes me to a side of it where I know the fishies do not bite. I want to say something but don't. Isaiah puts his rod in the water but there is no worm on it. Sometimes Isaiah is very strange indeed.

We are sitting there not catching any fish when all of a sudden we hear singing.

What's that? I say.

It's Indians, Isaiah whispers. Get down!

We peek around a boulder and sure enough there is a whole tribe of Chinooks and they are burying a dead Indian. A mamma Indian and her baby. It just about makes my own heart break looking at that tiny little baby swaddled up with its mamma. It gives me a real chill.

Isaiah whispers that they're Chinooks from over Deep River way.

An Indian funeral? I say.

I know how much you like adventures May Amelia, Isaiah says. Jane told me there was going to be a funeral so I thought I'd bring you here.

Jane is the Chinook wife of one of our neighbors. It is something indeed that Isaiah has gone to all this trouble for me, May Amelia, and I am not even a sheep. I have no doubt. This is a real miracle.

This sure is more exciting than fishing, I say.

There must be about ten Indians and they are all big and strong-looking. One of them is wearing oyster-shell necklaces and a white blanket with a black stripe. He seems very sad indeed and is crying over the poor dead mamma and baby.

They have the mamma Indian all laid out like she's supper or something what with flowers and baskets of fruits and trinkets and cooking pots all around her. She's wrapped in a blanket and lying in a big hollowed-out canoe with the baby cradled in her arms, and my, it sure is a tiny babe.

I say, Isaiah I sure hope they don't eat the lady, them being savages and all, and he says, Don't be ignorant May they're just honoring the dead with the fancy layout. They aren't fixing to eat her. See, she gets to take all those things with her to heaven. Watch May, they're going to set her up in the trees in the canoe.

Why? I say.

So that she can paddle that canoe right to the center of the Earth where heaven is; that's the Chinook way.

And sure enough they put the canoe on this wooden platform high above the ground, next to another platform that looks to have somebody on it too.

Jane says this place is called Mem-a-loose Shwalpeh, Isaiah says, Chinook Indian Tree Cemetery.

Why are there holes in the canoes? I say.

Jane says they put holes in the canoe for the rain to drain and also so that no one will steal it, Isaiah says.

I want a closer look at all this and wouldn't you know I step right onto one of mean old Kaarlo's traps. Kaarlo is always setting traps all about the homestead and even here on the Baby Island. One time Wilbert and I found a fox who had near-about chewed off its foot trying to work itself free of one of Kaarlo's traps.

When I step on the trap I let out a yelp that can be heard clear to Astoria, and all the Chinooks, well they hear too and come running and see me sitting on the ground crying, trying to get the trap off my leg. It hurts real bad, and it's only a small trap really, and I'm bleeding and Isaiah's trying to calm me down like I'm one of his sheeps saying May May don't you worry none May I'm gonna get you out of here safe and sound, you just calm down you hear me, you just calm down. Baa-baa-baa.

Isaiah is standing over me waving his fishing pole like he is a sheriff or roughrider or Wild Cat

Clark or I don't know what.

I can't get the trap open and I scream, Isaiah Get This Offa Me but he tries and tries and can't. One of the Indians, the Crying Indian with all the necklaces, moves Isaiah away and opens up the trap and I'm free.

It feels like a Real Miracle. I know now for sure what it feels to be a rabbit or beaver or whatever and I will never eat anything caught in Kaarlo's evil traps again. I do not care if I starve.

The Crying Indian tears off a piece of his blanket and ties it around my ankle and then picks me up and carries me to a long canoe tied up at the shore.

I say to the Crying Indian, Was that there your wife and little baby that died? but he just shakes his head; I don't think he understands Finnish. So I make as if I am cradling a baby in my arms and point back at the island and the Crying Indian nods sadly. Yes, they surely were his.

Isaiah points out our homestead up the Nasel. The Indians paddle smoothly and the sleek canoe is like a bird, it feels like it is gliding across the water, just skimming on the top. I think about how hard it is to row our little boat and I know that these Indians are strong men indeed to make this long canoe go so fast; why, they make it look like it is no trouble at all. Jane told me about these boats. She said they are called "dunking canoes" on account of them being so hard to handle; a person most often ends up getting dunked in the water.

I see our house and the little dock and I can just about make out Wilbert and Bosie. When we reach the bank Isaiah shouts, May's Been Hurt Come Quick! Mamma and Pappa and Ivan and Alvin and Matti and Wilbert and Wendell come racing to the Nasel and their eyes pop open when they see who is carrying me to shore but this big Indian.

What have you gone and gotten into May Amelia? Pappa asks with a heavy sigh.

Pappa goes up to the Crying Indian and holds out his arms and the Crying Indian puts me right into them.

Thank you kindly, Pappa says, for taking care of my girl here. She's a pack of trouble but she's the only May we've got.

Pappa smooths the hair out of my face.

The Crying Indian just nods and takes off one of his oyster-shell necklaces and puts it on my neck. And then he gets back into the canoe and they paddle away down the Nasel.

Isaiah says that the necklace means that I am an Indian princess, and maybe I am. When I am better I intend to go back to the Baby Island and put flowers on the grave of the mamma Indian and the baby Indian. Or on their tree anyways.

I sure am tired of setting here in bed waiting for my ankle to heal up. Mamma says I cannot play because it's likely to get infected. I am going right crazy with nothing to do.

Mamma says it is a miracle that the spikes did not break my bones and only cut me. She's been slathering one of her healing medicines on my ankle, spruce gum pitch and bear grease, and it smells something awful. Mamma has a way with healing, and she midwifes for miles around, going away for days at a time to catch a baby. She says that babies come when they are least expected and so it is not unusual for some poor man to be at our door in the middle of a storm on account of his baby deciding to get born without consulting the mamma. When Mamma is not here I must do all the cooking for the boys and Pappa—breakfast, lunch, and supper—and that is no fun at all.

Wilbert and Ivan and Alvin and Matti and Wendell and even Kaarlo come in to admire my leg.

That's a wicked-looking wound May, Wilbert says, envious.

Yeah, Alvin says. It looks like a real—

A real wound, Ivan finishes.

Isaiah told me you were very brave, Matti says patting my head.

It's awful though, I say. It's pink and nasty-looking and is starting to itch. And it still hurts.

It'll heal up fine May, Wendell says, sounding like a doctor. He peers at it through his glasses. I know something we can put on it to make it stop itching, he says, and runs out of the room.

I hope it will be okay May, Kaarlo says anxiously. He is no doubt feeling guilty since it was his mean old trap that got me and that is why he is being kind. It would be a miracle indeed for Kaarlo to be nice to me for no reason at all.

You should be proud to have such a scar on your leg, you look like a real soldier, Wilbert says. I suspect these brothers of mine have been listening to too many of Jacob Clayton's tales and their brains are addled.

Isaiah comes in with a wooden box and says, I'm really sorry your foot got hurt May. I intended the trip to be an adventure and it turned out a disaster.

That's okay. It's not your fault.

59

He thrusts the box out at me and says, Here.

I look in the box and cannot believe it.

Buttons the barn cat has had a new litter of kittens. They are tiny, small as a child's fist and their eyes aren't even open yet. The kittens are so soft and sweet and they are all sorts of colors. They're all crowded around Buttons, angling to get at her milk. Buttons gazes up at me contentedly, she is a proud mamma.

Mamma says, Those kittens have to stay in the barn but you can give them some milk every day.

But Bosie's allowed to sleep inside with Matti, why can't the kittens? I say.

Mamma says, May Amelia that cat of yours is just full of fleas and I suspect those kittens will be flea-ridden pretty soon too. I've just put fresh hay and duckfeathers in all our mattress ticking and I am not about to let those animals in and have them drop flea eggs everywhere, and that's all there is to it. She stays in the barn and those kittens too. They'll be plenty warm with all that hay to snuggle in.

But Mamma— I say.

Mamma ignores my whining and says, Isaiah Jackson get those animals out of here right this minute.

Isaiah takes the box out but when he returns he shuts the door and reaches into his pocket. He pulls out a tiny kitten. Its eyes are closed and it fits in my two hands, it is that small. It's got calico markings and it nuzzles against my hand.

I'm gonna call him Little Chief on account of the Indians we saw yesterday, I say.

That's a fine name, Isaiah says.

He's a real miracle, I say, snuggling the kitten.

Yes, Isaiah agrees with a smile.

Well, I say, there are miracles and there are sheeps, and we both laugh.

CHAPTER FOUR

No Kind of a Brother

There's no accounting for luck, especially luck in getting brothers.

It is nearly the middle of August by the time my foot heals and I am in the back pasture helping Wilbert when a girl comes stomping across our field.

All the older girls in the county like my handsome oldest brother Matti. They come from miles around, from Deep River even and in the rain sometimes, all dressed up with ribbons in their hair. They are trying to snag him for a husband.

This girl here is from pretty far away. I don't even know her, and she tries at smiling at me.

Hi May Where Is Your Brother Matti? she says, tossing her curls in my direction.

I know she doesn't like me because I am too

young not seventeen like her. These girls won't even talk to me unless I tell where he is which I usually don't.

She taps her shoe which has got manure on it from tromping in our fields and says, Well May, Where Is He?

I lie and say, I believe Matti has gone up the Nasel and sailed away with my Uncle Henry Smith the sailing captain haven't you heard?

But she knows I am lying and ignores me and searches around the front pasture until she finds him. I hate these girls. I could hit them.

Wilbert says, Ignore her May, she must be desperate if she's chasing after Matti like a cat in heat.

Matti is Pappa's favorite because he looks like Pappa did when he was a boy. My brother Matti is big and strong and his hair is blond as straw and he has smiling gray eyes and looks the way a real Finn should. He doesn't tease me like Kaarlo and is always telling Pappa that he shouldn't be so hard on me when I get into mischief. Matti is so nice but sometimes I wish he wasn't quite so nice because then these girls would stop coming around and bothering me about him.

I tell him so too. When the girl has left I find him. I say, Matti I don't believe one of these girls who has come calling is a real lady because Aunt Alice says real ladies let the men call on them which makes good sense when you think on it.

Matti just laughs and says, You are right May Amelia and I'll tell you something else. I don't like these girls much either. I already have a sweetheart but it is a secret and you mustn't tell anyone.

But why? Is she ugly or has she got the pox or something?

No she is beautiful but Pappa wouldn't like her because she's not a Finn. I have to keep it a secret. You understand May Amelia don't you?

Sure I do Matti, I say. If she's not a Finn what is she?

She's Irish, he whispers.

Now I know why Matti has not told Pappa about his girl. Pappa thinks that the Irish are nothing but trouble, always coming around and taking some Finn's job. Why, he says that even some of the gillnetters are now Irish. Pappa says the Irish are like locusts. And now Matti fancies one?

That's bad luck, I say.

May Amelia, I'm pretty sure that she'll be nothing but good luck for me, Matti says with a grin.

At supper Pappa says, Your brother Matti is going to live with Uncle Henry in Astoria for a spell and work on his ship. He'll be leaving in a week with Feenie.

When Kaarlo hears the news, his face gets all stormy and *Slam!* he's out the front door. Kaarlo has wanted to live and work in Astoria forever it seems. And now Matti's going, not him.

I wish Kaarlo was going away instead of Matti, I say to Wilbert.

Kaarlo has never been a good brother, maybe because he is really a cousin fostered over to us. Mamma is always saying Kaarlo may be your cousin but love him like a brother. Well that may be but Kaarlo is hard to love. He is always sullen and angry at everyone. He's not handsome like my brothers because he is always frowning. Kaarlo is forever teasing me and saying I am Nothing But A Pest. Wilbert says it's on account of the time I put tar on Kaarlo's pillow which I wouldn't have done if he hadn't gone and dunked my pigtails in the inkwell at the schoolhouse.

Pappa will have to let go of Kaarlo someday. It's natural for a boy to want to go away and find his fortune, Wilbert says.

Maybe Pappa will let him find his fortune real soon. Maybe he'll go to Alaska or wherever and get himself eaten by a grizzly bear, I say.

After I finish my chores the next day I watch Matti as he and Kaarlo fix the fence around the pen where the pigs live. Matti sees me and gives a big smile, his eyes light up and he says, Come and give us a hand May.

Kaarlo grunts when he sees me coming over.

Here, hold this down, Matti says, handing me a board.

Like this? I say, balancing the board between two posts.

Exactly May, Matti says. Matti is such a good brother, he's always helping me and teaching me things. He is teaching me spelling in English because he says mine is wretched and do I want to spend my whole life being able to write only in Finnish?

Matti uses both hands and a heavy mallet to hammer in his side of the beam.

Your turn, Kaarlo, Matti says, wiping his brow. This is thirsty work, I'll go get us something to drink. You stay here and help Kaarlo, May.

Okay, Matti.

Kaarlo fixes me with an eye and says, Hold It Steady May Amelia.

Inside the pen, the piglets are squealing. They

think it's feeding time. Maybe I will play a little trick on Kaarlo.

Kaarlo lifts his hammer back, and when he brings it forward I drop the board and it swings away. Kaarlo hammers right through the air and the weight of his swing hurls him into the pigpen, facefirst in the muck.

I feel glad my trick on mean old Kaarlo went so well. But he is up in a flash and has me by my hair and is shaking me like a sack of flour.

You did that on purpose, he says, spitting out mud.

I did not!

You weren't paying attention girl.

It slipped, I say.

Well, Kaarlo says, wiping the mud off his cheek, I guess I'm gonna slip too.

He picks me up and tosses me into the piggery where I land facefirst in the muck. Matti appears as I am pulling myself up.

Matti! I wail.

Matti sets down the refreshments and rushes over to the pen.

What happened Kaarlo? he says, taking in Kaarlo's muddy front. Kaarlo glares at Matti and says, I don't have to answer to you and stomps away, trailing mud.

68

Kaarlo threw me in Matti! I say.

Matti raises an eyebrow. Matti always takes my side, he is a nice brother, not like mean old Kaarlo.

You look like one of the piglets May Amelia.

I swipe at the mud on my face.

Come on out of there, he says, and let's get you cleaned up before Pappa sees you like this or there will be trouble for sure.

I stand next to the pump and he pours buckets of water over my head.

May, you gotta stop baiting Kaarlo. I'm gonna be gone soon and he'll be the biggest one so you'll have to mind him.

I cannot imagine minding Kaarlo.

But he's never nice to me! I say.

Well, sometimes you aren't too nice to him either.

But he's not even my brother, I say loudly.

Matti looks at me with disappointed eyes.

And he's not likely to forget that he's not a brother with you constantly reminding him May.

Kaarlo is Pappa's sister Aili's boy. When Aunt Aili and her husband Asmus came west, they had a real hard time, what with five children and a baby, and when they got to San Francisco they had to sell their luggage because they didn't have

69

enough money to get a railway ticket for the baby, who didn't even need a seat when you think about it, 'cause he rested on his ma's lap, but they had to buy one anyways. The family headed north and when they got to Astoria they borrowed some money from Pappa to pay for the boat fare on to Vancouver but they didn't have enough for Kaarlo. Since Kaarlo was ten and the oldest they left him with us where he has been to this very day.

Wilbert tells me that Aunt Aili is always writing letters to Kaarlo about how wonderful it will be when they can send for him, but they never do and that's why Kaarlo is always in such a bad mood. Kaarlo's folks must be real poor 'cause he's seventeen now and we're still stuck with him.

It is sad indeed but I suspect Kaarlo would be ill-tempered even if Aunt Aili had fetched him back long ago. Maybe they really left him with us because of his spiteful nature. He's not nice to anyone, not me or Wilbert or Ivan or Alvin or Wendell or Isaiah. Why he's not even nice to Matti who everyone knows is the kindest Jackson boy.

Kaarlo is really mad now and won't abide me to be near for even one second of the day. He still teases me and says that I am uglier than any boy he's met, even though he was the ugly one with slop all over his face. He is so mean, almost as mean as Pappa, but I don't let him see me cry I go out to the hayloft in the barn and cry there. Wilbert says Just Ignore Him May.

A few days later Wilbert, Wendell, Kaarlo and I have to go help out Uncle Aarno with his nets.

Mamma says, This isn't a convenient time for me to be lending you out right now May Amelia so be sure to be a help to your Uncle Aarno and then hurry on home.

Mamma can do less and less around the house. Her back is always paining her and Pappa says she's not to do any more lifting. This baby tires her out more 'cause it's been so long since she had one in her belly. Wendell says that she should rest which leaves me with all the work.

Uncle Aarno is a gillnetter, he catches salmon that swim in the Columbia. He uses special nets that tangle the salmon by their gills. Us children are to mend his nets and tan them so that they will last longer in the water.

Uncle Aarno lives down the Nasel, past the Smith Island and that is where he keeps his bateau, the boat he uses for catching the salmon. He also runs the mail boat, which is called the

OUR ONLY MAY AMELIA

General Custer, up and down these parts when he is not gillnetting. It is always a good day when we get a piece of mail from some relative far away. I often wonder how the letters travel all the way to get to our farm.

When we arrive, Uncle Aarno is on his verandah with some knitted flax nets, and I can tell from the smell that he is boiling tanbark on his stove. Uncle Aarno's house is very big and has the only full-round verandah in the valley. He bought the house after Eino Sjöblom killed himself, why Eino just hanged himself right there on the verandah. Uncle Aarno says that he sometimes hears the ghost of poor old Eino a-swinging from the verandah by his rope when it is still at night. It gives me a chill to think of him swinging in the wind.

Uncle Aarno told Wilbert that Eino Sjöblom was in love with a Chinook woman and she wouldn't have anything to do with him and so he killed himself. A sadder story I have never heard. Eino Sjöblom was famous around these parts because he was the first man to bring in a real iron cookstove. Wilbert tells me that he carried the cookstove for ten miles on his back.

Hello children, says Uncle Aarno looking up

from his nets and smiling. He is untangling his nets in the yard.

Uncle Aarno looks just like Pappa, only older and kinder, even though he is really younger. He has light hair and laughing eyes. He has no children of his own since his wife Saara died in childbirth years back.

Hello Uncle Aarno, Wendell says, are we knitting and dipping nets today? Everyone knows that Wendell has a good hand with knitting and mending the nets.

He looks at us children and says, Why boys that is certainly what we are going to do. Are you going to be helping, May Amelia?

I say, Yes I am Uncle Aarno, I can dip nets as good as any boy. Just you see.

What about your dolly there, is she going to help dip too? It's messy work you know.

No, Susannah is going to set on your verandah and watch us.

Kaarlo tries to scare me, he says, Tell your Susannah to watch out for old Eino swinging from the porch, that's what she should be looking at, not us.

Wendell says, Don't speak ill of the dead Kaarlo.

73

Yeah Kaarlo, don't speak ill or his ghost will surely come and haunt you, I say, being clever.

He'll see your ugly face first and be so scared he'll run away, Kaarlo taunts.

All right children, Uncle Aarno says, enough of that talk. There's work to be done and it sure ain't gonna get done by itself.

Uncle Aarno shows us how to take the nets and dip them carefully bit by bit into the boiled tanbark. The tanbark sets the flax so that the nets last longer in the water and are tougher. It sure is hard work 'cause the nets are really long and get tangled easily. The tanbark smells something awful and no matter how hard I try I end up getting more of it on me than on the nets. We spread the nets out to dry on the ground next to the house.

At lunchtime Uncle Aarno brings out some oyster fritters and *hätälepä*, Finnish quick bread. We set on the verandah and eat.

So May Amelia, Wendell says pushing his glasses up his nose, what are we going to sew for Susannah next?

Wendell is smart and clever and so good at sewing that he will surely be a doctor. Wendell says that there are schools back east where a person can learn doctoring. I think he should go away to learn doctoring but I think I will be very sad to see him go. Wendell is my favorite brother after Wilbert; he is good at knowing my mind.

I reckon a pirate suit, I say.

Is your dolly gonna be a pirate? asks Uncle Aarno. Why not a princess or a bride or something more ladylike?

That's boring, Uncle Aarno. Ladies and princesses don't get to have adventures because they get left behind. Susannah has got the taste for adventure like Uncle Henry. She wants to go to the East Indies and the Sandwich Islands too.

Your Uncle Henry's no pirate May Amelia except maybe to the Englishmen, Uncle Aarno says. A sea life isn't as exciting as you imagine. Nothing good to eat for weeks at a time and only smelly sailors for company.

May'll fit in just fine then, Kaarlo says with a smirk. She's about as smelly as they come.

Shut up Kaarlo, I say.

But Uncle Aarno, Wilbert says, sailors get to see the whole world; they can go nearabout any-where. Me and May are setting out to be sailors when we get old enough.

Uncle Aarno laughs and says I suspect it'll be a cold day indeed when Alma lets her girl go sailing around the world. But you never know children, it sure enough seems like the devil's land here on the old Nasel when the winter's biting through your socks. You never know when your bateau is going to freeze up now do you? You just never know.

Uncle Aarno has had an exciting life, although he says that all the excitement Darn Near Killed Him. He stowed away on a ship called the *Whistler* bound to America from Finland. The *Whistler* wrecked off San Francisco and he was one of only two men who survived. He headed up to Nasel where Pappa lent him some money to start gill-netting, what with salmon being so popular and the cannery in Astoria being built right around that time.

I liked his wife Saara and was real sorry when she died having the baby. Mamma says they did everything they could for her but nothing would stop all the bleeding, not cobwebs or Chinook teas or nothing. When Saara died Uncle Aarno was real sad and lonely. Pappa says that the old house is full of bad luck on account of Eino Sjöblom. I think he must be right—maybe old Eino's ghost doesn't want anyone else who lives in his house to be happy with a wife when he couldn't.

—◦—

We work hard all day and are cleaning up when dark storm clouds roll in. It starts to thunder and rain something fierce-like.

I guess you children will have to spend the night here, Uncle Aarno says. Your mother would have my hide if I sent you home in weather like this.

The house is huge and dark. It hasn't seen a woman's touch in a long time and it looks it. There's dust everywhere.

Where am I sleeping? I say.

You take the back bedroom May and one of you boys can bunk in with me and the other two can have the beds in the middle room.

The stairs are made from carved mahogany. My bedroom is at the very-most back of the house, at the end of a long hallway. It has a cold-looking iron bed with a dusty spread.

It doesn't look like he's cleaned since Aunt Saara died, I say.

At least you have a good view of the Nasel, Wilbert says.

Uncle Aarno hollers for us to come on down for supper. He has a huge pot of *mojakka*, fish chowder, bubbling. He ladles it out and we all

77

sit down at the table. He gives us big glasses of clabbered milk, and pours himself some home brew.

You sure are a good cook Uncle Aarno, Wendell says.

Mamma often says that Wendell is the only one of us children with a speck of manners. He always knows just what to say.

Do you ever get lonely out here all by yourself? I ask.

Nope, Uncle Aarno says.

Where did Eino Sjöblom sleep? Kaarlo asks rudely.

I eye Kaarlo. I am wondering if he has something up his sleeve.

In May's room, Uncle Aarno says, chewing carefully.

My room? I say. I can't take another bite, even though the *mojakka* is so creamy and good. In my room? I am not going to sleep a wink.

Uncle Aarno nods his head, it is the same way that Pappa nods.

I turn to Wilbert. Maybe you can stay in my room tonight, I say.

Are you scared May? Kaarlo taunts.

I ain't scared, I say.

Maybe you're scared of old Eino Sjöblom's ghost getting you? Kaarlo says, digging at me.

I said I'm not scared!

Then why does Wilbert have to sleep in your room?

He doesn't. I can sleep all by myself.

Well be sure not to have nightmares, Kaarlo says, smirking.

I want to punch him.

You can't scare me, Kaarlo!

Leave her alone, Kaarlo, Wilbert says.

Yes, and mind your manners, Kaarlo, Wendell says.

I'm lucky that I have real brothers who stick up for me.

Kaarlo takes a bite of chowder and ignores me for the rest of the meal, which is the nicest thing he's done all evening.

I am sound asleep when I hear the creaking. At first I think it is part of my dream.

Outside the wind is howling and the rain is falling in sheets. Then, over the wind and rain, I hear the creak. I don't recognize the sound. But I hold my breath and there it is.

Creak, swish, creak.

Wide awake, I pull my overalls on over my nightshirt and slip into my shoes and creep out to investigate. It's not coming from the other rooms; the only sounds out of them are snoring.

As I walk down the stairs, I can hear the creaking getting louder and louder. The shadows of the trees are dancing against the windows and look like ghosts. I wish Susannah were here with me.

Creak, creak.

Someone there? I say. I'm scared now.

But no one's answering me, just the creaking. And it's coming from the verandah.

I slip out the side door into the rain and wind. The creaking is getting louder now—I'm almost on top of it. I leap around the corner of the house, around the verandah, and there is something swinging away in the dark wind.

It's old Eino Sjöblom swinging from the roof of the verandah!

Aaaaaagh! I scream.

I run back into the house and up the stairs as fast as my feet will carry me to Wilbert, who is no ghost.

I burst into his room and with a pounding heart yell, Wilbert! Wake up! Wake up!

I shake him hard. He squints sleepily at me.

What's the matter May? he asks. I'm soaked straight through and must look a Real Fright.

Wilbert! Wilbert! Eino Sjöblom's swinging on the front verandah, I Just Saw Him!

Wilbert jumps up and we fly downstairs.

Kaarlo is already there and he's untying old dead Eino Sjöblom. He takes a look at me clutching Wilbert's hand and starts cackling. Then a clump of hay from Eino Sjöblom's hand falls to the floor.

But it's not Eino Sjöblom at all, it's just a scarecrow.

Kaarlo, Wilbert growls.

Kaarlo is laughing so hard he is doubled over. Not scared of anything, huh, May Amelia? Kaarlo says, gasping for breath.

I hate you, Kaarlo, I say, and stomp all the way back to bed.

He is no kind of a brother, that's for sure.

The next night me and the boys are back at our house. It is Matti's last night before he goes to Astoria with Aunt Feenie. I fix *laksloda*, sliced potatoes and salmon baked in milk sauce. It's very tasty and is Matti's favorite dish. Uncle Aarno gave me some Royal Chinook salmon which is the best kind. Everyone knows that salmon are the sure sign of a good fisherman and it is rare that Uncle Aarno has a bad day and catches plain old steelheads. His neighbor who is an old woman will call out to him Cleaning Steelheads Again Mr. Jackson? when he does, but yesterday he caught some salmon so I could cook us a special dinner for Matti.

Everyone is at the table, and I am just setting out the food when Kaarlo says, A bunch of boys are leaving for Alaska on account of the gold rush; I'd like to try my luck.

Pappa just keeps eating, doesn't pay him any attention at all.

The boys keep quiet and Mamma justs sits there, looking strained. I don't know if I should keep on filling up the plates or if I should stay where I'm at. I decide it's best to stay out of the way even though I want to say that I think it's a fine idea for him to leave.

It's a good opportunity, Kaarlo says belligerently. And besides Matti's getting to go to Astoria.

Pappa bangs his fist on the table.

Kaarlo, that gold rush is for fools with no sense, can't you see that we're barely making ends meet, isn't it enough that there's a new baby to feed you might as well just shoot your poor mother it'll be the same thing as letting her lose a son to some foolishness.

She's not my mother, Kaarlo says coldly. My real mother's in Vancouver.

Kaarlo! Aunt Feenie says with a gasp. Alma's practically raised you, how can you say such a cruel thing?

Mamma bends her head, and her hair falls over her slender neck like a waterfall on the Nasel, hiding her face. Why isn't she defending herself? Mamma never lets anyone talk to her that way.

I don't care, Kaarlo says fiercely.

Don't Speak In That Tone, Pappa says. His face has gone all stormy.

I look over at Wilbert and he shakes his head, a shake that says Keep Quiet.

Aunt Feenie says gently, Now Kaarlo don't be like that. You know Alma loves you. Don't be mean and say such unkind things.

Well, it's the truth, Kaarlo says standing up. He points at Mamma. She's not my ma and you're not my pa. I don't have to listen to you!

You do so! Pappa shouts. We're the only kin you have left in this world.

A hush falls over the room as the color drains from Kaarlo's face. Pappa puts his face in his hands. Mamma is weeping now, soft hiccoughy sobs.

What do you mean? Kaarlo whispers, like he doesn't want to know.

Aili's dead, Pappa says, his voice breaking.

The room goes dead quiet. It is so silent that all I can hear is the sound of Wilbert's stomach growling.

Finally Kaarlo asks in a stunned voice, My Ma's Dead?

And your pa and the children too.

Dead? All the kids?

They're all dead. They got the fever. Nearly half the town is dead.

When? Kaarlo says, his voice trembling. His face is white and he is shaking.

Six months ago.

Why didn't you tell me? Kaarlo's voice is so raw with anger I do not even recognize it.

We did what we thought was right, Pappa says, and he picks up his fork and starts eating again. Mamma is sitting real still, and there is a tear running down her face.

Kaarlo looks full of rage and sadness and suddenly pushes back his chair and runs out of the room as if a demon is on his tail. Pappa looks around at all of us. We are all still, even Bosie.

You children leave him be, you hear me?

Kaarlo hasn't been home all week.

We should have told him before, Mamma says, worried.

We did what we thought was right, Pappa says. I'm sure he's fine Alma, he's not a boy anymore.

I ask Wilbert where he thinks Kaarlo has gone off to.

He could've gone anywhere May. He could be halfway to Alaska by now, Wilbert says.

Now I'm thinking I was pretty mean to him, that maybe he ran away 'cause he thought he wasn't wanted or something. On account of me always saying he was no kind of a brother.

The boys are feeling bad too. Ivan and Alvin are convinced it is their fault for playing pranks on him. Matti is debating whether or not he should go away to Astoria and believes that the whole situation is his fault. Wilbert thinks he should have been kinder to Kaarlo. Isaiah is avoiding all us children and is staying with his sheeps. Wendell says there's no mending a torn heart, but he wishes he could.

It is a bad time indeed to be a Jackson child.

Finally, Aunt Feenie must return to Astoria.

I miss Henry, she says. He's been back in port

nearly a week now and will be wondering where I am.

But Matti doesn't want to go until Kaarlo's been found.

Pappa says firmly, Matti, don't let this stop you from going with your aunt. He'll turn up, you'll see. Pappa wants Matti to be successful.

I help Matti pack his trunk. He's just tossing clothes in, not folding anything at all.

Matti, I wish you weren't going, I say.

It's not very far, May, just Astoria.

I'll never see you.

Don't get all mopey, Matti says. I pick up one of the shirts that he's bundled in a knot and fold it properly. All of a sudden I can't take it. First Kaarlo and now Matti!

Please don't go! I say, hugging him and starting to cry. I promise I'll be a good sister, I won't get into any more mischief, you'll see. Please don't leave me here. I can't bear it if you go too.

Oh little May, Matti says, hugging me back tight and smoothing down my hair. You got a pack of brothers to look after you here. You won't even have time to miss me.

Yes I will, I say with a sniffle. You're My Only Matti.

Matti laughs.

Just remember one thing, May, Matti says, rubbing away my tears.

What?

He gives me a bright grin and ruffles my hair.

You're My Only May Amelia.

Jacob Clayton comes by our house after supper a few days later and visits a spell with Pappa. When he leaves he says, May Amelia, why don't you give me a hand carrying these pies your ma made for me back home.

Mamma has made three blackberry pies with berries Ivan and Alvin picked and given two to Jacob on account of him having no woman to cook for him.

Sure Mr. Clayton, I say, I'll help you carry these pies if I get a slice.

On the way back to Mr. Clayton's farm I tell him about Kaarlo running away and how bad I feel about it.

Where do you think he went? I ask.

Who could say May Amelia? Sometimes a body needs time to sort things out for himself.

When I open the door to Mr. Clayton's house, Kaarlo is right there, piling up wood by the fireplace.

I cannot believe it. Kaarlo has been right here, next door, all this time?

Come on, you two. Let's sit on down and eat this pie your ma made for us, Mr. Clayton says, as if Kaarlo stacking wood by his fireplace was an everyday occurrence.

Mr. Clayton carves Kaarlo and me a huge piece of blackberry pie. Kaarlo won't look at me but digs right into his pie.

I'm so nervous I don't know what to do with my very own self.

I try to take a bite of pie, but the words spill out of me.

Kaarlo won't you come home?

Kaarlo just stares at me, looking grim.

I know I was mean to you and I'm sorry, I say.

I hang my head like Bosie when he's been whupped. I ain't been any kind of a sister to you, I say.

Still Kaarlo doesn't say anything. He's never gonna say anything, he's never gonna come home even though we are his only kin and it's all my fault. I am remembering every mean thing I have ever done to him and when I get to the time I put lye in his bathwater I stop. It is too long a list.

I get up and say, Thank you Mr. Clayton I guess I'll head home now.

I have nearly reached the front door when I hear Kaarlo's voice.

Wait a moment May Amelia, Kaarlo says. It's dark out. I'll walk you home.

He gives me a ghost of smile.

Thanks, I say, I feel safer having a brother walk me home.

CHAPTER FIVE

Grandmother
Tries Our Patience

Everybody knows that I was the first girl to be born here on the Nasel, all the other mammas had boys including my own mamma who had six of them.

Mamma says, I swear to you May Amelia there is something in the very water that breeds boys, you are Simply A Miracle.

My grandmother does not think that I am A Miracle. That is, Pappa's mother, Grandmother Patience.

At breakfast Pappa says, Your Grandmother Patience will be coming to live with us on account of her getting on in years.

I swear I don't rightly understand why Pappa's letting her live with us, she's fit as can be, I say to Wilbert.

None of us children likes Grandmother Patience 'cause she's real mean and doesn't care for children. I don't know why she even had Pappa and Aunt Feenie and Uncle Aarno and Aunt Aili. She always says children are nothing but devils and demons.

She has a silver-tipped cane that she uses to walk and one time she whacked Wendell so hard that he had a bruise on his cheek for a whole week and all he'd done was talk back to her. I haven't seen sight of her since I was eight years old even though she only lives in Astoria. That time she yelled at Mamma, said she was no kind of a wife to my pappa, didn't know how to do anything right let alone raise seven boys and one scrawny girl, and then she took Mamma's favorite dish which Pappa had brought all the way from Finland and threw it at her and smashed it against the wall. After that Grandmother and Pappa had a real big fight and Grandmother Patience hasn't come back until now.

Wilbert tells me Grandmother Patience was poorly named.

When Grandmother Patience arrives she looks at Mamma real hard, from the top of her head to her big belly, looks her up and down like she's looking at a cow.

Grandmother Patience says, Alma, it falls to you to care for me in my declining years even though you have got yourself with child again I see.

Mamma sighs and says, Well, Mother Patience, you'll be staying in the sewing room. May Amelia and the boys have fixed it up real nice for you, and I sure do hope you'll be comfortable.

My mamma is a real strong woman. She had to be to have homesteaded here with my pappa when it was still a wilderness and there weren't any other families at all. But I don't understand why she lets Grandmother Patience have at her. Wilbert says he overheard Pappa say to Matti that the oldest child must always look after the parents, and that it was his bad luck to be the oldest.

Grandmother Patience walks back to the sewing room all slow with her wicked cane and looks into the room. Wilbert and I picked fresh flowers and put them on top of the dresser and a drawing I did in school of a cat is hanging on the wall, it is a good and decent drawing, even Miss McEwing said so. Mamma has put fresh linens on the bed and stuffed dried lavender under the mattress. It is a lovely room, smells real fine and has a window view of the Nasel.

We all hold our breath as Grandmother Patience looks around.

This room won't do at all, I'll take the one on the far end of the hall, she says like she is the queen.

Wilbert and I look at each other and he says Grandmother that's me and May's room don't ya like this one none?

Grandmother looks at Wilbert and says, I think it is a scandal that these two share the same room, boys and girls should not sleep together. From now on I shall sleep in the end room with May Amelia. Now that Matti is gone, Wilbert can have his place in Kaarlo and Wendell's room.

I look at Mamma and sure enough she knows that my life will be A Living Misery if I have to stay with Grandmother Patience and besides Mamma knows that Wilbert is my favorite, that I love him best of all.

Finally Mamma says evenly, Well Mother Patience, I suppose you can have the far room but the children will share the sewing room. I don't fancy May Amelia sleeping unprotected, being a young girl like she is, and I've already told her

94

how I want her brother Wilbert to keep an eye on her to see that she don't go getting herself into mischief and he won't be able to do that very well now if he isn't sleeping with her.

Grandmother Patience goes *Humph* and stalks off. Mamma looks at Wilbert and me and sighs.

Well children, she says, I suspect we're in for a real storm.

My poor brothers are gonna be carting and carrying for the rest of their days.

Grandmother Patience is insisting that they bring all her good furniture to our house and so they have to go down to Astoria and cart the furniture one half mile from her house to the boat, sail back to Knappton, cart it on a wagon and then onto the rowboat, and then finally carry it all the way into me and Wilbert's old bedroom. She's making them bring her heavy old rug, which looks like rats have been chewing on it, her own china, a big old bureau, a mirror, a night table, a washstand, pictures of her and Grandfather, and a small chair that she calls her settee.

Grandmother keeps saying that Mamma's furniture is No Good and that if she's going to live in the wilderness she wants to have Nice Things around her. All her furniture is musty-smelling and dark-looking, nothing like the furniture Isaiah makes.

I honestly don't know how you live like this Jalmer, Grandmother Patience says to Pappa at supper.

Pappa just grunts and keeps eating the fish-head stew, it is his favorite Finnish food. It tastes okay I guess, but I mostly try to avoid the eyes.

And your daughter is just a hellion, says Grandmother Patience, fixing me with her evil eye. Why you wouldn't even know there's a girl under that dirt. She's filthy.

Grandmother looks me up and down.

And she's wearing trousers. It's scandalous, she says.

That's because I've been mucking out the barn, I want to say but Wilbert kicks me hard under the table, a warning kick. There's no arguing with Grandmother Patience. I bite my tongue.

Jalmer, you should send this child to the Our Lady School to learn how to behave.

All us children gasp, even Kaarlo.

Mother Patience! Mamma says.

The Our Lady School in Astoria is run by mean nuns. Every child knows that the nuns beat the children with switches and make them sleep in cold beds and eat only gruel.

Pappa raises an eyebrow and says It's a Catholic school Mother. I'm not sending my daughter to a Catholic school when we are Lutherans and besides even if I wanted to we can't afford the fees.

Well I see that you won't listen to good sense so I suppose I must take it upon myself to school May Amelia in how to behave, Grandmother Patience says ominously.

I do so know how to behave, I say.

You are an ill-mannered slovenly girl. And you dress like a street urchin, Grandmother Patience says.

Well you're a Mean Old Witch! I shout before Wilbert can stop me.

Enough! Pappa says, banging his fist on the table. I work hard all day and I want to eat my supper in peace! Not another word out of anyone.

Grandmother Patience curls her lip meanly at me, and I just know that I am going to pay for what I said.

Wilbert and I lie in bed and listen to Mamma and Pappa fighting about Grandmother Patience.

Goddammit Jalmer, I do not want that woman in my house, Mamma says.

Well she's here and we have to make the best of it.

That woman has been here two days only and she's already turned everything upside down. She's no help at all, just more work and another mouth to feed.

She's my mother and she's staying and that's final, Pappa says.

Mamma says, Your mother is nothing but trouble.

And then they lower their voices and we can't hear them anymore.

Do you think Pappa will send Grandmother away? I whisper to Wilbert.

Nah, he whispers back, she's stuck here like a cow in the tidelands.

And we're the fly on her back I think.

Grandmother Patience is the devil. I am convinced.

Grandmother Patience whacked me so hard on the shoulder with her cane that when I undress for bed there is blood all over my undershirt and under the blood a big old bruise the size of a hen's egg.

98

Wilbert says GoodLordMayAmelia, what the heck happened to you?

I say Don't you go cursing at me Wilbert Jackson, I just don't wanta hear it.

I am tired of being yelled at all the time now. Grandmother Patience says that I am No Good, that girls are Nothing But Trouble. I don't know if she means all girls or me in particular. She says I am a wicked wicked girl and that I have spiteful eyes. I know in the Bible it says that it is a sin to wish for someone's death but I cannot help but wish that Grandmother Patience would simply go ahead and die and leave us all in peace. I surely must have done something mighty awful to deserve her but for the life of me I cannot imagine what.

Wilbert says, Come on May what happened lemme see your shoulder. Good Lord did some boy beat you up? Tell me who did this to you May and I'll whup 'em good, me and the boys will get 'em I swear.

I say, Wilbert you ain't gonna be whupping nobody 'cause that mark is from the witch sleeping in our room.

Grandmother Patience?

Wilbert sits back down and shakes his head. His hair is all ghostly in the candlelight.

What happened?

I was in the kitchen by myself getting supper started when she came in and began saying she had some mending she needed done. I said I couldn't do it, the boys were due home any time and I had to have supper on the table. Then she just whacked me. Said girls are meant to obey and that she'd whack me again the next time I talked back to her.

He says, I cannot believe Ma and Pa let her live here and treat you the way she does, it ain't right. I know we're supposed to respect our elders but she doesn't deserve a speck of respect, that mean old witch. Well I'm gonna do something about it.

Wilbert sneaks upstairs in the still of the night and steals Grandmother Patience's cane while she is sleeping and gives it to Bosie who I'm sure has it hid somewhere beneath this house and she will never find it.

For every evil God sends to me he sends an angel and I know sure for certain that Wilbert is my guardian angel.

A few days later Wendell and Wilbert and Ivan and Alvin and Isaiah and Kaarlo and me are downstairs minding ourselves. It is late, after supper, and Mamma and Pappa have gone over to visit with Lonny's parents for a spell.

The boys and me are all worn out from a hard day of bringing in the hay. We always bring in the hay in September and this year is no different. It is very hard work indeed because we have to wait for a day without rain. If the hay is wet, it will be no good and will rot. When we woke up today the sun was shining, so Pappa yelled at all us children to get a move on out to the fields. We even borrowed Lonny and Jacob Clayton to help and they will get some hay in return. Even so, we still have a lot more to bring in tomorrow.

Wendell is helping me sew a new dress for my china baby doll, the one Aunt Feenie gave me. The doll is sitting in the rocking chair. We are trying to make an Indian dress but it is quite tricky and I suspect we will have to ask Jane for some help.

Ivan and Alvin and Kaarlo are reading quietly. I have sewn together the pages of the Finnish newspaper, the *Amerikan Suometar*, so that it will not fall apart being passed around. It is the only Finnish newspaper we can get out here and it is fine indeed even though it is often two weeks late on account of how far it must travel to get to our farm. Isaiah is snoring in the corner, he is all tuckered out after bringing in the hay and then checking on the sheeps. He works harder than all us children some days. Wilbert is trying to mend a shoe that Bosie got ahold of and chewed. It's a real mess though and there's no saving it I think. Bosie whines at Wilbert like he knows he did something wrong.

Bosie you sure are a dumb dog, Wilbert says.

Wilbert, I say, you can't leave anything lying around.

That was my good pair of shoes. Now I'll have to borrow an old smelly pair of Kaarlo's, Wilbert grouses.

Kaarlo looks up from the paper and gives Wilbert the eye but even he's too tired to start a fight.

Grandmother Patience comes stomping down the stairs. She sits heavily on a chair and says, May Amelia, go on and fetch me some tea. She is fingering her new cane, a twisted rough-hewn stick. Where did she get that?

I go on out and make up some tea for her.

Here's your tea, I say.

She takes a quick sip and frowns. It's not even hot, she says. Make me a new cup, this one's no good.

It is so hot I nearly burned my fingers. I want to say No! but Wilbert fixes me with a look, a look that says Just Do What She Says and so I go back into the kitchen anyway and make another cup. It is steaming hot this time, with a little trail of smoke.

It's hot, I say, handing her the cup.

She takes a sip and purses her dried-up lips in a nasty smile.

Didn't you put any honey in at all girl? It's not a bit sweet. Can't you do anything right? Take it away and bring me another, she says meanly. I swear you are the most useless child in the entire house.

The boys are watching us. Ivan and Alvin have stopped reading the paper. Wendell has put down his needle, and Isaiah is awake now and observing quietly from the corner. Wilbert is watching every word that comes out of Grandmother Patience's horrible mouth and I think that even Kaarlo feels sorry for me. I wish Matti was here, he would never have let her do this to me.

My blood is boiling like the tea water, I want

103

to throw this cup in her face but Wilbert gives me a wink, a wink that says Pay Her No Mind. I swear I don't know what I'd do without Wilbert. I go back on out to the kitchen and pour three whole spoonfuls of honey into the tea, the very last bit of honey in the jar. Mamma says that Grandmother Patience has eaten up every sweet thing in this house.

Grandmother Patience takes the cup from me and sips it slowly and we all hold our breaths. One, two, three. She licks her lips and looks around at us children.

This is terrible tea, she says. It's not sweet enough and it's cold. Make me a fresh cup immediately.

I just stand there.

She bangs the floor with her cane. But I've had all I can take.

There isn't any more honey you Greedy Old Witch! I shout.

She stands up to her full height and shakes her cane at me. She is big, bigger than I thought and she is full of fury. Her mouth is twisted in an evil snarl.

How dare you defy me, you little brat, she says. Go And Make Me A Cup Of Tea.

I won't! I say.

Wilbert and Wendell stand up at the same time like they are going to do something but this seems to infuriate her more.

Fine, she says. Have it your way, you evil child.

And time seems to stand still as she raises her wicked new cane in the air at me, and I flinch away, but she swings it with all her might and brings it down hard, not on me but on my beautiful china baby doll sitting in the rocker, smashing her into a million pieces.

I cry myself to sleep.

When I wake up it is dark and I'm cold; my teeth are chattering.

I am cold every night it seems now that summer is gone no matter how many flannels I put on me or the bed. Wilbert complained this morning at breakfast that my chattering teeth kept him up half the night.

Mamma said she was making a new quilt for us on account of ours being threadbare but that it would be spring before she'd be finished. She can't get a stitch sewn with the baby kicking at her all the time.

The wind is whistling in the room. I think of my poor broken baby doll and whimper, I am so cold and sad.

Wilbert whispers, It will be all right May.

I don't think it will ever be all right again.

I roll over and shiver some more. I am the saddest coldest sorriest girl ever. I wish I'd never been born.

And just when I think my bones have frozen into place Pappa comes in. I am afraid I am in trouble, that Grandmother Patience has blamed me for the broken baby doll somehow. I cannot bear it and pretend to be asleep.

Pappa sits down on the bed and brushes the hair back from my cheeks. He sighs heavily and says, I sure am sorry about your baby doll May Amelia.

I just lie there, still as a mouse. And then I shiver. Pappa leaves the room and a moment later he is back. He lays his good tweed coat on me, the warmest coat ever, it smells so fine, like an open field, or the breeze blowing off the Nasel.

This'll keep you warm my little May, he says. After all, you're the only May we've got.

And wouldn't you know, I am as warm as any

of Buttons' kittens, that big old tweed coat of my pappa's keeps me warm as a summer day and I say, I believe you are right, Pappa, I believe I am the only May you've got.

CHAPTER SIX

How to Be a Proper Young Lady

It seems like everyone is conspiring to make me a Proper Young Lady.

Our teacher Miss McEwing who is young and nice and always has a kind word has even started on me. She is not a Finn and doesn't know much Finnish at all. She has come all the way from Pennsylvania to teach us children. I cannot imagine why she wants to be here on the Nasel but Mamma says we are lucky to have anyone at all. Wendell says that she is sweet on Ben Armstrong on account of her always visiting him and bringing him pies and such.

Now that it is October and the harvest is in we are back at the schoolhouse.

Why all the Jackson children are here. This is certainly a miracle, Miss McEwing says.

Miss McEwing is forever saying that the Jackson children are the tardiest in the valley. We often miss school because of the farm. That and the boys not liking school very much at all, except Wendell. Wilbert has the hardest time and is always getting into fights with the other boys at the schoolhouse on account of them teasing him about his white hair. They are real mean to him and call him Whitey Wilbert. Pappa says that Wilbert must go to school to learn and not to fight.

We finally got the hay in, Wilbert says.

Well now that you are all here let's move on. What do you children want to be when you grow up?

I want to be a sailor, I say.

A sailor! Miss McEwing exclaims. She seems shocked.

Yes indeed. I am gonna travel with my Uncle Henry, he is a great sailor did you know? I suspect I will travel to faraway places like China and whatnot.

Well, that's quite exciting May but do you think your family's going to want a young lady like you traipsing all over the world? Why don't you stay here in Nasel and be a teacher like me?

Why would I want to stay here in Nasel? I don't want to be stuck here forever. You know I've been reading and there sure are a lot of places to go in the world.

But May Amelia, Miss McEwing says, Proper Young Ladies don't go gallivanting around the world on ships.

Well I sure ain't no Proper Young Lady Miss McEwing, you can ask any of my brothers here.

And every child starts laughing and Wilbert laughs so hard he falls off his chair.

Miss McEwing tries to look serious, but finally her eyes crinkle merrily and she laughs too.

No matter what Miss McEwing says I do not think being a Proper Young Lady sounds like any fun at all. Why everyone knows that Young Ladies must stay home all the time, and do embroidery and keep clean. I think I would have the hardest time with the keeping clean part. I get dirty quick like the boys. Boys have more fun, there's no two ways about it.

Why, Wilbert says that he has gotten work upriver at Ben Armstrong's logging camp and I cannot think of a better thing. He is going to help out on the splash dam. The logging men make a dam across the river and put all the cedar logs they intend to get downstream behind the dam. The Armstrong dam is a big one, Wilbert says it's fourteen feet high and forty feet at the base. When it is time for the splash dam to be released, a whistle sounds and the dam is opened—the water floods out, and the logs with it. It can be real treacherous.

The Nasel is real rough and wild high up near the logging camp so when the splash dam is opened, the logs pop clear into the air and shoot down the Nasel, flying dangerously downstream until they end up in the bay by our house. Then the logs are rafted downriver to the boom where they are sorted and stored before going on to the Sunshine Mill. They must sag the Nasel after the splash dam is released. Sagging is when the men clean up all the logs that get stuck in the banks or on folks' farms.

Usually some boy must run down the Nasel and warn all the families that they are sending down the logs. Otherwise you never know, somebody might be doing their washing in the Nasel or setting a line to fish or taking a bath and when they look up here come all these logs barreling downstream. Sometimes Ben Armstrong hires Ivan or Alvin to be the boy who runs and warns everybody.

When I was small child, Lonny Petersen was playing in the Nasel and his ma didn't know he was there and they opened the splash dam and the logs came down and he was swept down the Nasel and banged up by the logs. He was hurt real bad and Mamma says He Almost Didn't Make It. Pappa says he reckons that's why Lonny hasn't been right in the head since.

Pappa says, May Amelia you listen for the boy who tells you that the logs are a-coming down the Nasel, you don't want to end up slow in the head like Lonny, now, do you?

Wilbert is going to be a Whistle Punk, the boy who gives the whistle that it is time to open the dam. It's a very exciting job.

I wish I could be a Whistle Punk like Wilbert.

They'd never let you, Wilbert says. On account of you being a Young Lady and all.

It's not fair, I say.

Mamma overhears me and says, May Amelia, you are not supposed to be working the splash dams with the men. Proper Young Ladies simply don't do such things. Lord knows there's nothing more dangerous than that logging camp, between the accidents and fires. It's a miracle they get any work done.

I wonder about Mamma sometimes. Mamma is

a lady but not the usual kind. She is very strong I know on account of helping Pappa run the farm all these years and organizing the boys. She has a mind of her own and doesn't hesitate one bit to give you her opinion. Wilbert says she is as tough as Pappa, but just has a kinder way of showing it.

I look at Mamma's belly and something is pushing the front. She lets me touch her belly. The little baby's kicking and it feels like kittens tumbling.

Mamma, I say, that little baby in your tummy is wrestling like Ivan and Alvin.

She says, May Amelia, I believe you are right.

Grandmother Patience comes clomping into the kitchen and gives me a mean look. She won't talk to me anymore, not since Mamma yelled at her for smashing my baby doll. Mamma said that Grandmother Patience Went Too Far and that if she was going to stay in our house, she'd have to abide by Mamma's rules and That Was That.

Hello Mother Patience, Mamma says.

Grandmother Patience caresses her wicked cane and eyes me like she wants to takes a swing.

Mamma looks between the two of us and just sighs. She knows there's gonna be trouble for sure.

Cut my hair Wilbert, I say.

Have you gone crazy May? he says.

Cut off my hair, that way I can get a job with you up at Ben Armstrong's. If I wear my overalls I'll look like just another boy.

But you're a Young Lady May, you heard Mamma.

Don't you start too Wilbert. I never get to have any fun like all you boys, it's Not Fair.

I don't know May, Wilbert says, shaking his head.

If you don't help me I'll do it myself.

Fine May, Wilbert says. I'll cut it off.

And snip-snip, my long brown hair is gone.

I go up to Ben Armstrong's camp. I have to sneak out of the house so Mamma and Grandmother Patience won't see my hair. The men are getting ready to send a load of logs down the Nasel. It is dangerous work indeed, and so they have brought in Lars the Swede to tell them how to do it properly, to show them how to construct the splash dam. Lars the Swede is an old man but he is a real expert. He was a bridge maker in Sweden until he married a Finnish girl and came

115

to America. He has the fiercest eyes with pointy brows and a great white beard that Wilbert says he got from scaring children.

Lars says, Hello May Amelia what are you doing up here? We don't usually get young ladies a-calling.

I want a job, I say.

Well I don't know about that. We have plenty of help right now with the cooking, what with Nora Fuller and Mrs. Petersen lending a hand since your Aunt Feenie left.

Not cooking, I say, exasperated. I have to do that at home. Maybe I can be a whistle punk, I suggest.

A whistle punk? Lars says looking puzzled.

Yes, like Wilbert.

I don't think your pa would be too happy about that May. We don't generally hire on young ladies as whistle punks.

But there's got to be something, I say.

Lars scratches his head thoughtfully.

I suppose you could be the child that runs on down the Nasel and sends the warning, he says.

I say Sure, sure, fine. I can run fast as any boy, just watch me.

Lars laughs and says, You look like a boy with

116

that hair of yours. I believe you can run May Amelia, I've seen you run away from those brothers of yours when you've gotten into mischief.

How much will I get paid? I ask.

Lars rubs his beard like he is thinking seriously. One penny seems fair, he says.

Fine! I say.

All right, Lars says, get going May Amelia. Go run on down and let the good folks know that logs are a-coming so that we don't send logs crashing into their Sunday washing.

And so I run and run down the Nasel, down past the Widow Katja Krohn's farm and Jacob Clayton's. It is a long stretch along the Nasel, and in the distance I can tell that they have released the splash dam, that the logs are racing down the Nasel with me, and are almost catching up.

The Dam Is Open! Logs a-coming! I holler as I run past every person, but I don't stop I keep going because the logs are simply shooting down the river. I reach the Petersen farm and Lonny is in the field and gives me a wave.

Hi Kaarlo, he hollers to me and I stumble realizing that Lonny has mistaken me for Kaarlo on account of my short brown hair.

I get up and keep on going, I run until I am

nearabout out of breath and then I am back at our house and Bosie is jumping and yapping at my feet, wanting to play.

Bosie go lie down, I say. No tricks today—I'm all worn out. It's heaps more fun not being a Proper Young Lady.

Tonight is the dance at the Finnish Hall for all the Young Ladies and Gentlemen. There is a dance every fall, after the harvesting's done. But I am not allowed to go and have to stay home with Mamma and Pappa and Grandmother Patience and Bosie and Buttons while all my brothers get to go, even Isaiah. Pappa is making him take a bath so he doesn't smell like a sheep.

But I'm a Young Lady, I say to Mamma. Everybody's been telling me so. Why can't I go?

Young Ladies don't look for work at logging camps and cut off their hair, Mamma says. Mamma is real upset with me.

But when your hair is up in a knot it looks short too. What does it matter? I say.

You don't look like any Young Lady I've ever seen, Grandmother Patience says meanly. You look a fright.

Mother Patience, Mamma says exasperated.

I say It's Not Fair. Wilbert's going and he's no gentleman and neither are the rest of the boys.

Mamma shakes her head and says Just Be Patient, May Amelia. There's time enough for boys.

I say I'm not interested in boys, I just wanta go to the dance.

No, May, Mamma says firmly, and goes back to crocheting a blanket for the new baby with bearbone hooks. It is clear that I am going to have to sit at home with the animals and grown-ups and have no fun at all.

The front window is open and all of a sudden a seagull flies in through it, flaps madly around, and then flies out with a loud squawk.

We all freeze.

Every Finn knows that it is bad luck for a bird to fly into your house and die. It means that someone in the family will die. Finally I break the silence.

It surely was alive when it left, I say.

Yes indeed, Mamma says, relief in her voice.

The girl's right, Grandmother Patience agrees.

We all laugh nervously.

It's just superstition anyway, Pappa says.

It may be superstition, Mamma says shakily, but it certainly gave me a scare.

119

She pats her round belly, looks over at me, and sighs.

The boys had to milk the cows and then walk all the way to the Finnish Hall for the dance on account of the Nasel being plumb full of logs. The Hall is a long walk past the tidelands on the way to Knappton. There is always a lively time to be had at the Hall, and it is where all the wedding feasts and parties are held.

Pappa said that the boys had best be back by dawn for milking time or there'll be the Devil To Pay.

And sure enough, those brothers of mine barely find their way home by the time the sun is peeping out over the valley. I am downstairs in the kitchen when they sneak in. All the boys are real cranky on account of getting no sleep at all, especially Kaarlo.

I see you are home just in time for the milking, I say.

Kaarlo fixes me with a sour look and says, Go away, May Amelia. You're a sorry sight after a night of dancing with Tyyni Honko.

Bosie's nicer-looking than that horrible Tyyni Honko, I say.

At least she's a real lady, not like you May Amelia with that hair of yours, you don't even look like a girl no more. You're no kind of Young Lady.

Even mean old Kaarlo wants me to be a Young Lady.

Well you're no Gentleman I say.

Pappa comes out and says That's Enough Stop Bickering and get to your chores.

And that is that.

Later that morning Lonny comes by and his eyes go all wide. What happened to your hair, May? he says.

Wilbert cut it off.

Oh, he says. My cousin Thymei needs some help harvesting the cranberries. Do you and Wilbert wanta come?

Lonny's cousin Thymei has cranberry bogs and he sells cranberries back east where they are very popular. He lets us children pick the cranberries, and we get a penny a bucket. Some of the boys call Thymei One-Eye on account of a mean old bull goring out one of his eyes. Not me though, Thymei is mighty big and has a real fierce temper and I stay outta his way.

It's quiet now that the hay's been brought in

121

but I have to be back to fix supper. Mamma's been feeling bad all morning.

Sure Lonny I say. I'll round up some of the boys.

Isaiah won't leave his sheeps and Wendell is collecting herbs and no one can tell for sure where Ivan and Alvin have gone off to. So just Wilbert, me, Kaarlo, and Lonny head out to Thymei's cranberry bogs.

It's a fierce autumn day, the kind that lets you know that winter is just around the corner. It is wet and cold and all misty like. The bogs are on the Nasel upriver maybe three miles away. Kaarlo is skipper.

Kaarlo says, This weather is awful I can't see a thing on the river.

Logging makes the Nasel real hard to navigate sometimes. Why logs and broken branches will pile up and overnight there will be snags where there weren't any before and that's the end of your boat.

We round a bend and Wilbert says, We're not too far now.

Kaarlo is not right about much, but he is right about this weather. It is certainly awful and the closer we seem to be to the bogs the farther away they seem to get. It's all foggy and thick but real quiet, the only sounds are water lapping and scraps hitting our boat. Wilbert and Kaarlo start fighting over who gets to be skipper on the way back home.

Wilbert says, You always get to be skipper Kaarlo, it's not fair.

I'm older, Kaarlo says.

Well if I'm going to be a sailing captain I need to practice at navigating.

But it's only the Nasel, says Kaarlo, not even the Shoalwater Bay or the Columbia.

I take Wilbert's side and say, Wilbert's gotta practice Kaarlo even Uncle Henry says so.

Kaarlo says, Shut Up May Amelia what do you know about anything anyway, you're Just A Girl, not even a Proper Young Lady. Besides you always take Wilbert's side.

We tie up the boat and have to walk for about one half mile and the fields are soggy. When we reach the small stream that leads to Thymei's bogs, we see that it is a rushing river on account of the rain and there is no way we can cross it on the log bridge. It's been washed clear away.

We'll have to go up and take the swinging bridge, Wilbert says, and then loop around back down.

123

Everywhere in the Nasel valley along the rocky steep areas where boats cannot go and the waters are too rough there are swinging bridges. The swinging bridges are made of thick rope and rough planks and are suspended over the water. They are ever so helpful on account of the fact that the log bridges can be awful slippery when it is wet and many a child including me has slipped off a log and into the cold water below.

We walk all the way up until we reach the swinging bridge. It is an especially long bridge which Thymei put in some years back and some of the planks are rotted out in places. The fog is so heavy that we can't even see across to the other side.

That fog's as thick as soup, Wilbert says.

I'll go first, Lonny says. I know the bridge.

Hold on to the ropes May, these planks aren't so good, Wilbert says.

Lonny creeps out onto the bridge and me right behind him. The ropes are slippery in my hands. Wilbert's right behind me and Kaarlo behind him. It's pretty windy and the bridge, hanging high over the water below, is swinging and swaying.

Don't slip on this bridge, May, Wilbert says looking at the raging water below. Otherwise we'll be fishing for girls.

124

I hold tight to the ropes.

We are nearly halfway across the bridge when Lonny, who has been quiet the whole way says, I hear a baby crying.

Everyone knows that Lonny isn't quite right in the head so Kaarlo says skeptically, A baby all the way out here?

Hush Kaarlo, Wilbert says. Listen.

Sure enough, through the rain and fog comes the clear tinkly sound of a baby crying from the other end of the bridge.

Well I'll be, says Kaarlo. It surely is a baby. Come on, let's keep moving.

Maybe someone abandoned it, says Wilbert as we creep along.

What's a baby doing way out here? I say. Why would anyone bring a baby out on a—

Will you shut up May how can anyone get a thought out with you chattering, says Kaarlo.

We need to fetch it, says Lonny, his voice lost in the swirl of wind. Lonny has always had a soft heart. One time he nursed back to health a sparrow that had broken its wing.

Yeah, says Wilbert. It'll die for sure if it's left out in this cold rain.

The baby's crying is getting louder and louder.

Why would a baby be all the way out here? I say. There ain't any folks around here, and it sure for certain don't belong to Thymei.

Be quiet May, Kaarlo says. You're just A Girl, what do you know about anything anyway?

No wait listen, I say. Remember what Wild Cat Clark told us, how—

But Lonny is moving closer to the other side and the baby's cries are right in front of us. A fierce wind comes up and swooshes the fog and we can finally see, not a baby at all, nothing lying there small and pink like little Moses in the rush cradle, no, not that at all. We freeze where we stand, still as deer at the sight on that bank.

And it comes to the boys at once, what I was trying to tell them, what Wild Cat Clark had told us. Wild Cat Clark, the legend of the valley, the greatest hunter, who'd caught and trapped with the best Chinook trackers, who kept a tamed wolf as his hound, and who'd seen an elk the color of snow high in the mountains. They remembered what he'd told us late one night last winter when we sat around the kitchen after he had taken the boys hunting.

I once heard a cougar cry like a baby calling for its mother.

126

'Cause standing on the bank is no baby.

It's a cougar.

Nobody moves. We are trapped in the middle of the bridge.

The cougar starts growling low in his throat, no more baby crying sounds. No, he looks mean and thin and hungry. And I imagine we look like supper.

Run! I shout and we all turn around and start to run back across the bridge.

Ahead of me Kaarlo and Wilbert are moving fast as they can, as fast as the wind will let them and so am I. I am nearly halfway across when I hear Lonny calling me, saying May May Don't Go May Don't Leave Me May. I look around and Lonny is right where I left him, he has not moved an inch, he is frozen with fear, staring at the cougar. I run back and sure enough he is frightened to death, big old tears are rolling down his cheeks, and so I push him hard, in front of me, and say, Go Lonny!

Lonny starts rushing across the bridge.

The cougar is still growling on the bank, any minute it will be on the bridge and it will be Good-Bye May Amelia, Hello Supper unless I do something.

I push Lonny forward.

Kaarlo and Wilbert have made it to the other side and they are hollering Hurry May Hurry!

I push Lonny as hard as I can ahead of me but all of a sudden the bridge gets the best of me—my foot breaks a weak plank and I go tumbling through. I grab the ropes.

Lonny! I scream.

Lonny turns around and sees me dangling from the rope and the mean cougar growling at us and he picks me up and tosses me over his shoulder like a sack of flour, barreling across the bridge. The cougar lets out a roar like nothing I've ever heard, worse than Pappa and Grandmother Patience put together and gathers itself to leap at us.

Come on Lonny! I holler.

And the mean old cougar leaps at us and it lands right on the broken part of the bridge, its big old paws just about on the broken planks. It hesitates for a minute, sensing trouble. I get an idea.

Rooaaaaar! I roar at the cougar.

The cougar's eyes narrow and it pounces forward intent on making a meal of me. But it is too heavy and the rotted-out planks break, collapse, and the cougar goes tumbling down with the loose planks into the raging water below. When it hits the water it lets out a roar. I wouldn't like to be the fisherman who catches that cat in his nets.

Lonny plops me down on the ground.

I cannot catch my breath.

That was close, Wilbert says, shaking his head at me.

Maybe next time you'll listen to me when I'm right, I say glaring at Kaarlo. Even if I'm not a Proper Young Lady.

Kaarlo eyes me and says, You're not right about much, May Amelia, but I have to agree, you sure don't look like any kind of Proper Young Lady I've seen.

I've lost a shoe in the river from my fall and my sleeve is all ripped. I'm wet as can be and I'm a real fright.

Well then, I say, I reckon it's a Darn Good Thing I'm not a Proper Young Lady or you'd be that cougar's supper right about now.

Kaarlo starts laughing real hard.

Yeah, May Amelia, I reckon you are right about that.

CHAPTER SEVEN

Bad Days Indeed

Wilbert says there are some days that are so bad there's no mending them.

I am thinking this is one of those days, what with having forgotten my dinner pail and my lessons. I went hungry at noon and got scolded by Miss McEwing.

Ivan and Alvin and Wilbert and Wendell and Kaarlo and me are on the little boat. Isaiah stayed home from school today on account of one of the sheeps having a bad leg. Kaarlo has fetched us home from the schoolhouse and he is in a terrible mood. But I'm ignoring him and telling Wilbert my troubles.

I say Wilbert, this has been a bad day.

We are on the Nasel near the bend by Lonny's farm and I say, Wilbert, why am I having this bad luck?

Kaarlo who is in a mean mood says, Hush Up May Amelia I'm tired of you always chattering, Can't You Ever Be Quiet Girl?

Kaarlo is always in a mood it seems since Matti left. A bad one.

I say, I hate you Kaarlo you're Always Awful to me and Kaarlo says, Shut Up May Amelia or I'm gonna put you on that snag over there and leave you for the monsters.

It is a terrible snag on the Nasel, made up of scary-looking brambles and slimy green wood and all sorts of muck.

Wilbert sticks up for me and says Yeah Kaarlo, stop being mean to May Amelia, she ain't done nothing wrong.

Yeah Kaarlo, Wendell says, leave May alone.

Leave May alone, Ivan and Alvin say together which is strange because they usually don't take anybody's side except each other's.

Shut Up All Of You, Kaarlo hollers.

Wilbert says, You're just in a temper because Tyyni Honko won't talk to you no more.

Kaarlo's eyes go all dark and stormy and he lets fly at Wilbert.

No fighting between brothers, I say, but they don't pay me no mind, me being only a sister and all. The boys are always fighting it seems and today is no different, even Mamma says it's what they do best. They bang and push around the boat and shove me and sure enough I fall right into the Nasel.

The Nasel is ever so cold in November, I cannot tell you how cold. It is not a good time to take a dip.

It seems to take forever for us to get home and by the time we get there I am frozen straight through and shivering so hard that I think for sure my teeth will fall right out. Wilbert carries me into the house.

Pappa is in the kitchen with Mamma and he takes a long hard look at us and says, Have you children been wrestling on that boat again how many times have I told you No Wrestling On The Nasel? Just look at May Amelia, soaked straight through, how did this happen?

Grandmother Patience eyes me with distaste and says, That daughter of yours is nothing but a walking disaster. Just look at her!

Pappa ignores her and says, Well? What happened?

It was an accident, says Wilbert real quick and fixes Kaarlo with an eye.

Ivan says, Yeah Pa it was an accident.

133

Boat wasn't balanced near proper enough and we hit a snag round the bend and May Amelia went tumbling in, Alvin finishes.

Those twins sure are sneaky.

Well how about that, Pappa says skeptically. Imagine a mean old snag getting the best of May Amelia Jackson.

Yeah, says Ivan, it must be May's snag.

And now all the boys are calling that snag by Lonny's farm May's Snag and Wendell has drawn up a map of the Nasel and put May's Snag on it and brought it to me where I am in bed on account of the dunking I got in the Nasel. Mamma has put a mustard plaster on my chest 'cause I am coughing so much. She says I need to rest and get better, that my cough sounds real bad. Pappa comes by and I ask him if I can take the boat out when I am better and he says No!

It's not fair, I say. The boys get to take the boat out.

That's why they get to take the boat out May Amelia, Pappa says. Because they are boys. Do you want to end up on the bottom of the Nasel? We're living in the wilderness and it's a dangerous place, May Amelia, and you girl have a got a Nose For Trouble.

Pappa stomps away. Pappa is always so unfair to me all on account of Being A Girl. Maybe if there was another girl around he wouldn't be this way. I hope for the hundredth time that I get a baby sister.

I sure do hope my luck gets better.

But things do not get better, they just get worse. Wilbert says that the Jackson family has no kind of luck.

A few days later when I am up and feeling better, the *General Custer*, the mail boat, is tied up on our dock when we get home from the schoolhouse. We only get mail a few times a month in these parts, usually depending on Uncle Aarno's mood.

Uncle Aarno just brought the mail out a few days ago, Wilbert says, what's he doing back here?

Uncle Aarno is sitting at the kitchen table with Mamma and Pappa and Grandmother Patience.

Hi Uncle Aarno, I say, excited to see him.

Hello there May Amelia, Uncle Aarno says. But there is no laugh in his voice and he is not in a joking mood like he usually is with us children, even his mustache appears to be drooping.

What's going on Pa? Wilbert says.

135

Your fool of a brother Matti was at Mariah's tavern last night in Astoria and now he's gone missing. Shanghaied. Aarno believes he is on a ship right now intended for the Orient.

Shanghaied? Ivan and Alvin say in disbelief.

Our Matti? I say.

That's certainly one way to travel the world, Wendell says shaking his head.

You're sure, Uncle Aarno? Kaarlo asks skeptically.

That's what I'm thinking, Uncle Aarno says, tugging at his beard. The boy has just plumb disappeared.

What are you gonna do, Uncle Aarno? Are you gonna track him down? I say.

Can't track down what nobody's seen, he says sadly.

I cannot believe that Matti has gotten himself shanghaied, I tell Wilbert. He's too smart our brother Matti.

Wilbert says, You sure don't know much about boys May Amelia.

I know plenty, I say. There are enough of them around here.

You sure don't know about girls, then. I bet the Widow Mariah herself had something to do with

136

it. She can be sweeter than maple syrup when she puts her mind to it, smart or not, Wilbert says.

The Widow Mariah is real notorious in these parts because she's the only woman who owns a tavern. She's got long white hair that she wears in a braid and it nearly reaches the back of her knees. Best of all, she smokes a pipe and keeps her money in her stocking high on her leg and thinks nothing of hiking up her skirt and pulling down the stocking for a coin.

She's famous for shanghaiing men who drink in her tavern. Wilbert tells me she'll slip something into their glass that knocks them out and then let them down a ladder to a rowboat waiting below where they're rowed out to a ship. When they wake up, they're far out at sea.

The trouble started when Mariah had her own husband shanghaied for ten dollars. Rumor is that when she slipped him down the ladder into the rowboat he fell into the water and sank to the bottom of the bay and drowned and she told everyone he was killed by pirates. Uncle Henry says that all the folks in town know the truth but it doesn't stop them from going to her tavern because the fritters are so good.

The next day Wilbert and I are trying to cheer up Bosie in the yard. Bosie is a good dog, but he's not very smart and he's real stubborn too. He usually only listens to our brother Matti. Otherwise he just does as he pleases. Wilbert tells me Bosie thinks he's a person. Matti was his favorite and he has been a sad dog indeed since he left. Matti used to save Bosie scraps every supper and sometimes breakfast too. Now Bosie is moping around the table and whining real sorry like and Pappa has banished him from the house until he learns to behave like a normal dog but he still howls through the door. He is feeling very sorry for himself.

I know that Mamma and Pappa are worried something fierce about Matti. I worry too but mostly I just miss him.

We are passing a ball back and forth but Bosie is in no mood for tricks and instead takes a bite out of Wilbert's overalls and runs off with it. I suspect he intends to hide it under the house with the rest of his treasures.

Bosie got you good Wilbert, I say, laughing at Wilbert's overalls.

All of a sudden Bosie runs back and he's yelping and barking real excited like and there is

Lonny's ma running and crying and stumbling down the trail through the woods that leads up to the logging camp. She is hysterical for sure and her hair has fallen all around her head and she is saying Mayamelia Mayamelia Fetch Your Mamma, Mayamelia Fetch Alma Ohmylord.

Mamma is in the kitchen making biscuits and has flour all over her apron.

Mamma Mamma hurry something's the matter with Lonny's ma! I say.

When we go outside Wilbert is sitting next to Mrs. Petersen with his arm around her patting her back, and Mrs. Petersen is crying her very heart right out.

Calm yourself Ida. What's the matter for goodness' sake? Mamma says wiping her hands on her apron.

Nora's dead! Mrs. Petersen wails.

Nora Fuller's dead? Dear heavens what happened?

She's been murdered! Split right open like a slaughtered animal you cannot believe the sight ohmylord Alma the blood everywhere look at me I have blood all over my apron I got Nora's blood all over me we gotta sew her up she ain't got no kin round here we gotta put her together

139

we can't leave her there like that all falling outta herself!

Mrs. Petersen cries and cries, and Mamma clutches her big belly and looks real white.

She says, Wilbert, take Mrs. Petersen home and put her straight into bed. May Amelia go fetch your pa and the boys and tell them to get home quick, I said so.

Wilbert helps Mrs. Petersen up and then leads her down the path to her house.

Mamma says, Go on May do as I say.

And so I run and run as fast as I can to round up all the boys, first to Pappa out in the south field and then to Isaiah in the back pasture with the sheeps and then to Ivan and Alvin and Wendell down by the tidelands and finally on to Kaarlo in Jacob Clayton's back pasture. By the time I get back all the boys are standing around the table listening to Mamma tell Pappa.

Who did it to her? Pappa says.

No one knows for sure. They suspect it was a loggingman, Micah Andersen, he's gone missing. Ida says that Micah fancied after Nora and she wouldn't have a thing to do with him.

I'm not surprised she ended up like this, Grandmother Patience says nastily.

Mother Patience! Mamma says.

What did she expect working up at a logging camp with a bunch of wild men? A real lady wouldn't have set foot in that camp, she says giving me the evil eye.

Pappa just looks hard at Grandmother Patience and says, Come on boys, we have got to fetch Nora and bring her back here and let your ma tend to her. Her kin's in Nova Scotia and she ain't got no one else to speak for her.

So my Pappa and the boys go to fetch Nora.

Nora Fuller's body is in our front parlor at this very minute, it is just lying on the couch waiting for Isaiah to finish building a box to hold it.

I didn't know Nora very well, but, my, she looks real terrible I cannot say how very terrible. Dead people do not look very happy at all.

Mamma and Mrs. Petersen are sewing her up with a big thick needle and Pappa's black fishing twine.

Mrs. Petersen keeps leaving and throwing up until finally Mamma says, Ida I'm the one with a babe on the way and I cannot stand being around sickness more than once a day so kindly leave me

141

to finish here. You aren't a speck of help in the state you are in. This girl needs putting back together, and it's never gonna happen with you hovering and retching.

Mamma says, May Amelia, fetch your brother Wendell for me. He has a good hand with the needle and thread.

Which is the truth for sure but the last time I saw him sew it was to make a new dress for Susannah. Who would've thought he'd be stitching up Nora Fuller?

Pappa is worried about Micah Andersen being out and around and he says, May Amelia, don't you go out to the pastures till Micah's been found, you understand me? Take a hard look at that poor woman lying in our parlor. You don't want to end up like her, now, do you? And no sassing me about wanting to take the boat on the Nasel—you're not going anywhere unless you got one of the boys with you. Wilbert be sure to mind May Amelia, see that she don't go wandering off dreaming like she does.

So now Wilbert is stuck to me like my very own shadow and all the boys must carry their guns.

I wonder where Micah Andersen has gone to,
I say to Wilbert.

The sheriff from Astoria and the men from Ben
Armstrong's camp are looking for him, he says.
They'll never catch Micah. These woods are too
big—nobody knows them 'cept Dead Men And
Indians. It's easy to disappear.

Jacob Clayton comes by and shakes his head.
First Matti and now this. My, we sure are living in
some bad times when a man will do such a thing,
he says.

Pappa says, Yes indeed, Jacob, times sure have
changed. These are bad days indeed.

The luck just gets worse.

Bosie has been whining every night since Matti
left and finally his enemy, the big mean raccoon
who lives behind the milking barn, hears him
going at it and they get into a terrible fight. The
raccoon bites Bosie real good and when we go
down for breakfast it's clear he is a beaten dog.
His cuts are bloody and nasty-looking and his
eyes are glazed.

Bosie looks bad Wilbert, I say.

Mamma says, I don't have medicine for
animals. You best take that dog of yours over to

143

Jane. Maybe she can mend him.

Jane is a Chinook princess, and she is Old Man Weilin's wife. Everyone knows that the Chinooks have a way with healing. Why, when Wild Cat Clark was just a young man, he shot himself in the leg while cleaning his gun and the Chinooks found him and nursed him through the whole winter. Wild Cat Clark always says that Chinooks are the best neighbors a fella can have, that they sure keep warm houses that smell real fine. He means the split cedar lodges, the kind that Jane has.

Wilbert bundles Bosie into a sling and we carry him over to the Weilin homestead. Wilbert and me go around back to where Jane lives. Old Man Weilin says he can't tolerate having a woman in the house and that's why he built on the other house for his wife. Wilbert says that Old Man Weilin is just plain crazy.

Jane seems pretty content to me in her own house, which is a Chinook-style lodge of split cedar logs. There are woven rush mats on the floors and a warm fire in the center of the room. Her place is clean and has a nice smell to it.

Jane is very pretty with long black hair parted down the middle in braids and big brown eyes.

Jane speaks real good Finnish. She's been trying to teach me the Chinook jargon but I am not a very good pupil. She is busy weaving a basket when we knock on the door.

Hi Jane.

Hello May Amelia, Wilbert, Bosie, she says, nodding her head.

That's what I like about Jane, she even says hello to our mangy dog.

The raccoon got him, Wilbert says.

He certainly did, Jane agrees, inspecting Bosie.

Jane is always kind to animals. She says the Chinook believe that souls come back as birds and beasts, so you must always treat them with kindness and respect.

Can you fix him? I say. Bosie looks pretty bad.

Why don't you leave Bosie here with me and I'll see what I can do.

Will he be okay? I say.

May will you let Jane have a look, Wilbert says, making me sit down on the rush mats so that Jane can tend to Bosie.

Did you hear? Our brother Matti's been shanghaied! I say.

That's terrible May, what bad luck.

Yeah, nobody knows where he is. I suspect he is in the Orient.

Bosie gives a low sad whine.

Is Bosie gonna be okay, Jane? He's been in a bad way ever since Matti left. Matti was his favorite person.

Jane shakes her head sadly.

An animal has to have the will to live, she says.

And looking at Bosie and knowing that he's missing Matti, I'm not real sure that he does.

I sit on the stairs and listen to Jacob Clayton talk with Mamma and Pappa.

Any word about Matti? Mr. Clayton asks.

Aarno hasn't heard hide nor hair of him, Pappa says.

A real shame, Mr. Clayton says. He'll turn up— don't lose hope.

Pappa just says *Huummph!*

Least he's not dead, Mr. Clayton says. The O'Casey girl, Mary, from way downriver, has gone missing.

That Irish family? Mamma says.

They think she might have drowned in the Nasel. She took a boat out by herself a week ago and hasn't been seen since.

The poor parents, Mamma says. She was their only girl, too. I can't imagine.

Well, her parents are real anxious to find her body and give it an honest burial, so tell the boys to keep an eye open on the river.

They have gathered all the gillnetters in the valley along the Nasel, and they are dragging the river from here to the Smith Island with their nets to see if Mary O'Casey's body turns up. Kaarlo and Ivan and Alvin are out with the gillnetters, lending a hand.

I sit on the dock by our house and watch them. The Nasel, usually so clean and clear, looks dark and cloudy from the dredging and I cannot imagine being on the bottom, like Mary O'Casey, on the bottom where it is black forever. I toss a stick into the water and the strong current sucks it swiftly away. I remember how Matti would toss a stick in the river and Bosie would jump in and fetch it for him. Bosie wouldn't do that for anyone else—he'd just sit there and look at you as if to say go on in and Fetch It Yourself. And now Matti is gone. I can't believe ole Bosie is sick and might die and Matti's never coming back. I am the saddest girl in Nasel.

There's got to be some way to turn the bad luck around.

Wilbert, I say, why don't we try and catch Micah Andersen?

Have you gone plumb crazy like Olaaf Kuula? Wilbert says.

We know these woods real well, I say.

May Amelia get that fool idea outta your head right now. Micah Andersen is a Wanted Man, and he already sliced up one woman.

But Wilbert—

No May and I mean it. Pappa's right about this one.

I can't believe Wilbert is siding with Pappa, and him being my best brother and all.

I discuss the situation with Buttons in the barn.

What do you think Buttons? Do you think I can catch that mean old Micah Andersen?

But Buttons isn't much interested in what I'm saying, she just wants to have her ears scratched.

It's clear as can be that I'm gonna have to do it alone. I sneak out of the house early in the morning before everyone else is up for chores. It's Saturday and there is no school. I take Wilbert's gun. Even if he misses it, I know he won't tell on me. Not Wilbert.

I take the trail that leads up to Ben Armstrong's logging camp. It's real early but all the logging men are already up and working and there is hollering everywhere. It doesn't make good sense that Micah Andersen would hang around here after committing such a Horrible Crime so I start up a path that I know leads away from our valley and to the other side of the mountain. Us children are forbidden to go to the other side of the mountain but that seems plain silly, it's not as if there's gonna be anything on that side that's not already on this side. It takes me until noon to get to the top of the mountain, and the view from the top makes my heart pound real fast. Why, a body can see everything from there—the Nasel, our farm, the Petersen farm, and Jacob Clayton's too.

Well, I say to myself. If I was Micah Andersen, I would surely hide on the other side of this here mountain. The other side is a thick woods, dark-looking and scary even. Exactly the sort of place a murdering scoundrel would hide.

I start down the slippery slope and there, beyond a big old pine tree, are two small baby cub bears.

They are as cute as can be, all roly-poly. I go over to the cubs. They see me coming and they flop on their backs for me, all playful like. The smaller one nuzzles my hand and I give it a good scratch on its belly.

You sure are the cutest animals I ever did see, I say. The cub does a little flip and I laugh.

And you're just full of tricks, why I bet you could be in the circus, I say.

All of a sudden I hear loud growling and it's not coming from the cubs. I turn around slowly and hear a roar. It's the mamma bear and boy is she ever mad!

The little cubs run on over to her but she doesn't pay them any mind, she's got her sights fixed on me, May Amelia Jackson. She takes off at a tear toward me and well, I'm just so scared that I drop Wilbert's gun and scramble up that old tree as fast as I can. The mamma bear is trying to get up the tree after me but I'm a real good climber and I go higher and higher and finally she lets out a roar and falls back down to the ground. I have heard that bears are real good climbers too but this one doesn't seem much inclined to doing it.

And now I am stuck in this tree and cannot get down on account of the mamma bear and her cubs sleeping at the bottom. I suspect she is waiting for me to come on down so that she can eat me. I have no luck at all it seems.

It's really dark. The stars have been out for a long time. I am so cold that my teeth are chattering. I cannot tell what time it is and I'm getting awful tired of setting in this tree. I cannot fall asleep or else I will surely fall off this branch and into the mamma bear's big teeth.

I wonder if anyone is missing me, if they've even noticed I'm gone. I bet they don't miss me one bit. Why would they care if a no-good girl's disappeared, one that's always getting into trouble. It sure is spooky in the woods late at night; there are all sorts of weird sounds. Jane always says that the bad spirits walk around at night and make animal noises to trick people. I sure wish I'd listened to Wilbert and wasn't stuck in this tree waiting to be eaten by a bear.

I must have fallen asleep in that hard old tree 'cause I wake up and nearly fall off the branch I'm on. I can see spooky-looking lights in the distance, and they are just dancing through the woods. I hope it's not old Eino's ghost tracking me down 'cause I cannot escape from the tree, that's for certain sure. They get closer and closer, why they are heading right at me! It's not enough that the bear's gonna get me, but do the mean old spirits have to also? The mamma bear starts growling low in her throat and then I hear a shot and the mamma bear and her cubs turn tail and run. It's not the spirits at all—it's a whole posse!

May Amelia Jackson you get down outta that tree right this minute! Pappa hollers. He is holding a torch and Jacob Clayton's next to him with a smoking gun.

I slip-slide down the tree as fast as I can. I've never been so happy to see Pappa in my whole life. And he's got everyone with him, all my brothers and Uncle Aarno and Mr. Petersen and Ben Armstrong and the sheriff and even crazy old Olaaf Kuula. Why, he's got practically the whole valley with him.

How'd ya find me?

One of my men saw you sneaking by the camp earlier today, Ben Armstrong says. He suspected

152

you were headed up the mountain.

I was trying to find Micah Andersen, I say.

All the men start laughing.

Girl we've been searching for you half the night! Pappa hollers. What were you thinking of, scaring us all like that with your foolishness? Why I've half a mind to send you to the Our Lady School just to keep you in one piece!

Pappa's real mad; his eyebrows are twitching and his lips are all tight together. A storm is brewing; I'm gonna get whupped for sure. I want to run but the sheriff is standing behind me and he has his hand on my shoulder to keep me from bolting I suspect.

Well Jalmer, now that your girl here is safe why don't we head on home? It's nearly sunrise, the sheriff says.

Sure enough, the sun is peeping out over the mountain. Pappa looks hard at me and there is a gleam in his eye. I wonder if I'm gonna get my backside tanned in front of all these folks. There is a moment of silence while Pappa scratches his beard thoughtfully. And then he says, Everyone come on back to the farm. May Amelia's cooking a breakfast for all of you!

153

The men let out a cheer and Wilbert turns to me and shakes his head. He knows I hate cooking more than anything in the whole wide world. It is a fitting punishment indeed.

You sure got your work cut out for you, May Amelia, he says.

I guess, but they haven't had my cooking before, Wilbert, I say and we both laugh and set off down the mountain.

We are nearly back at the house when all of a sudden I hear barking.

Bosie!

Bosie comes running over, yelping and jumping around and licking my face; he sure is glad to see me. His cuts are all bandaged.

Get Down Bosie, I say.

Jane's coming down the trail.

He's better now, Jane says, smiling.

Come on Bosie, I say and run over to the Nasel with him. I toss a stick into the water and Bosie just sits there and stares at me.

Same old Bosie, says Wilbert, and we all laugh.

After breakfast I sneak out and give Bosie some scraps of bacon. He is so happy that his tail is just a-wagging. He rolls around in the dirt at my feet and his bandages get all dusty. I think my luck has finally turned around.

You sure are a dumb dog Bosie, I say.

Bosie barks at me and wags his tail.

But you're the only Bosie we've got.

CHAPTER EIGHT

Mothers Grow Up Young Here

We are on our way home from Sunday service at the Rukoushuone, the Nasel Prayer House. Old Man Winter has arrived in the valley, and he is in a bad mood indeed. It is freezing cold. The Nasel is frozen over in parts and the air is icy. Everyone keeps saying that it is the coldest winter anyone can remember.

We are near May's Snag when Mamma's hand flutters to her belly and she says, Jalmer, you best get me home. This baby has decided it wants to be born this very minute.

Pappa goes all pale and says, Right Now?

Mamma says Isn't it Just Like a Jackson baby to want to get born on a boat on the Nasel?

I can hardly believe that the baby is finally here. It has taken just about forever for it to decide to get born!

You're gonna have the baby right here? I say. In this boat?

The baby doesn't know we're in a boat May Amelia, Mamma says with a weak smile.

All of a sudden there's a pool of water at Mamma's feet.

This baby's coming fast! Mamma gasps.

Wendell and Wilbert and Ivan and Alvin and Isaiah grab up all the oars that there are. They row and row as fast as they can. They almost resemble the Indians who saved me in the canoe.

Faster! Kaarlo hollers, acting like the skipper.

We're going as fast as we can! Wilbert shouts back. But he's not mad at Kaarlo; he is just worried about Mamma who is not looking too good. Mamma's breathing hard now, huffing and puffing and moaning. Our house is still nearly two miles away.

I'll never make it home Jalmer, Mamma cries.

Pappa, I say, let's go to Lonny's sauna. It's closest and it'll be warm.

Good thinking May, Mamma says, patting my hand. I knew I could count on My May.

When the boat reaches the shore Kaarlo jumps off and ties it and Pappa carries Mamma to the bank.

May Amelia, Mamma says on a moan, go and fetch Mrs. Petersen.

My clever brother Wendell who wants to be a doctor has turned pale.

Wendell Jackson, you stay here with me, Mamma says. If you want to learn doctoring, now's as good a time as any.

Wendell looks real shaky but nods.

So Pappa runs Mamma with her big belly heaving all the way to the sauna. Wilbert and Ivan and Alvin and me run ahead of him to the Petersen house while Kaarlo and Isaiah tie up the boat. The Petersen place is a ways back and when we reach it we don't bother knocking on the door, we just run right in.

Mr. and Mrs. Petersen and Lonny are sitting down to a nice dinner of roast duck, and it looks mighty tasty.

Hi May, Lonny says.

Mamma's having her baby! I say.

Where? Mrs. Petersen asks.

In your sauna!

Mrs. Petersen stands up, calm as can be, and says, Lonny, run out and fetch me some water.

Mrs. Petersen and me run down to the Nasel to the sauna.

159

Alma? Mrs. Petersen calls in through the sauna door.

She's right here, hollers my Pappa banging open the sauna door. A waft of cedar smoke hits my face.

Ida! Mamma wails at Mrs. Petersen.

Jalmer, why don't you go on to the house and set with Oren. We'll be a while here I think, Mrs. Petersen says, nodding at my pappa. Go on!

Pappa comes out looking gray.

May, take your pa on up to the house, Mrs. Petersen says, closing the door. And make sure Lonny brings me that water right away. Oh, and send down Wilbert with some towels too.

Behind the door Mamma is groaning.

Come on, Pappa, I say, grabbing his hand and pulling him up the slope. I have never seen Pappa like this before.

We walk to the house, where Mr. Petersen is waiting for us.

Oren, Pappa says nodding at Mr. Petersen. Sorry to disturb your dinner.

Pull up a chair and have something to eat, Mr. Petersen says. And I think some vodka too. Never can tell how long it's gonna take for a baby to come.

160

Thank you kindly Oren, Pappa says, taking a glass of vodka. Pappa takes a big gulp and some of the color returns to his cheeks.

Well Jalmer, Mr. Petersen says with a hearty laugh, the oldtime Finn doctors always said the best babies were born in the sauna, so there you go!

Baby Amy is the prettiest little baby I ever did see, with her duck-feather blond hair and bright blue eyes. Mamma says it was only right that I got to name her on account of me being her only sister and all. I ended up naming her Amy because it's MAY all mixed up. I named her second name after Aunt Alice just like I said I would so her full name is Amy Alice Jackson.

Mamma has been in a real bad way since having the baby and Aunt Alice has come up from Astoria to lend a hand. She says it is because Mamma is too old to be making babies. Mamma took a fever after Amy was born and it has been left up to me to take care of the baby while Aunt Alice takes care of Mamma. I am staying home from school to help with the new baby.

It is a lot of work taking care of Baby Amy, but I don't care at all because now I have a sister, I will never be alone again. She is a real live Miracle come true.

Baby Amy is crying so bad I fear she will split right open like Nora. She sucks so hard on my thumb that it is as wrinkled as the old Widow Krohn. I am beside myself; I don't know what to do.

The baby won't stop crying, I say, and Pappa says, Don't bother your mamma, she needs her rest.

But she's crying!

The babe is only hungry and that is all, Pappa says. Your mamma isn't strong enough to give the babe any milk and so we shall have to get some help from Old Liz the cow.

Pappa takes a piece of oilskin and hangs it in a cone and straps on a teat to it like I have never seen before. It is an amazing teat, like a real woman's, and I ask him where he got it.

Why, he says with a laugh, we got it when you were born. Don't you remember feeding at it?

No, I surely do not remember any such thing, but I believe him.

Pappa puts warm milk from the cow into the oilskin and I hold the teat to Amy's mouth and right away the babe latches on and sucks and sucks.

Ivan and Alvin and Wilbert and Wendell and Isaiah and even Kaarlo come around and watch me feed Amy with the milk teat and they say, My May Amelia, you sure are a good little mother.

Why look how that babe is drinking away—you sure do have a way with babies, Wendell says.

I believe I do have a way. At least with this baby.

Baby Amy is the most perfect baby I ever did see. I am making a record of her growings because Mamma says that's what she did when Matti and Isaiah were born.

What about Wilbert and Wendell and Ivan and Alvin and me May Amelia? I ask her. Didn't you keep records of all us?

No—she smiles weakly—any amount of children after two doesn't leave you any time to remember your own name let alone when they took their first step.

Mamma is not feeling any better, and is still in bed so it is up to me to keep a record for Baby Amy. Well, I am going to keep a perfect record so that when Baby Amy is grown up she will say, Why I had the very best sister, May Amelia, she kept a record for me and everything.

THIS IS THE RECORD OF
AMY ALICE JACKSON
Born on November 23, 1899,
on the Nasel like May Amelia.
Blue eyes like the boys.
10 fingers. 10 toes.
Drinks from Pappa's milk teat.
Enjoys sleeping all day and crying and
fussing when hungry for the milk.
No teeth to speak of.

This is all I can think of to say. Babies are not very exciting, but they sure are a whole lot of work. This one likes to eat all the time and always needs changing and none of the boys will change her, but I wouldn't let them anyway. Amy likes to sit with me in the rocking chair which Pappa has brought in to me and Wilbert's bedroom, and be rocked and look out the window at the Nasel going by real slowly. I tell her stories and she listens, looking up at me with her big blue eyes a-blinking away.

I say, Baby Amy, when you are grown up you and me are going to have such a wonderful time. You will be best friends with Wilbert like I am, he is the best brother and you will be my very best sister, and I know you'll be so very pretty—I can already see you in a robin-blue dress like Aunt Alice wears with shell buttons down the front.

Oh Baby Amy I wish you would hurry up and grow so that we can tell secrets and play hide 'n' seek with Bosie and catch fishies on the Baby Island and everything.

You must hurry up and grow Baby Amy for there is so much to do.

I am not the only girl around here anymore.

I am in the kitchen with Aunt Alice helping her fix biscuits for supper. She is wearing a pretty calico dress and it has got grease and flour all down the front of it and she even has a speck of grease on her face. Mamma still has the fever. It's strange to see Aunt Alice in our kitchen. I know she is a fine cook but she doesn't look like a lady who spends a lot of time in the kitchen.

I don't know how my sister does it, Aunt Alice says, wiping her brow. Taking care of this big house, feeding all those brothers of yours, managing the farm, and now a baby on top of it.

Baby Amy's no trouble at all, I say.

No trouble at all? she laughs with amazement. May Amelia Jackson that is a fib if I ever heard one. That child is nothing but work. Why, I don't think you've let her out of your sight since she was born. And I know she keeps you up half the night with her crying, just look at those circles under your eyes.

She's my sister, I say. I hafta look out for her.

And you're doing a very good job. You're a real help.

Grandmother Patience stomps into the kitchen. Her face goes all dark when she sees me standing there.

How are you feeling, Mother Patience? Aunt Alice says carefully. Aunt Alice knows all about Grandmother Patience from me and Mamma.

My leg is acting up, Grandmother Patience snaps.

I have a poultice you can put on it, Aunt Alice says soothingly.

Grandmother Patience stares at me.

It's acting up on account of the lack of sleep I'm getting with the babe up all night crying her heart out. May Amelia, you must be neglecting that child. All it does is cry.

Now Mother Patience, you know very well that May Amelia is doing a fine job with the baby.

If she's doing such a fine job then why does it

cry all the time? No good's gonna come of her looking after the babe. This girl doesn't have the sense that God gave her. Why, look at her.

Mother Patience, you aren't helping here, Aunt Alice says, her voice going up a notch.

Grandmother Patience hits the floor with her twisted cane and I flinch. This girl is not taking care of the babe! she shouts.

Alma's sick! And I have my Hands Full with her and the boys! Aunt Alice hollers back.

Then I shall care for the baby, Grandmother Patience says.

There is no way I'm letting Baby Amy anywhere near the old witch. She'd think nothing of taking the cane to her when she cried, I bet.

Mamma told Me to take care of Baby Amy, not You, I say.

Alma's not in her right mind, Grandmother Patience says, dismissing me.

Pappa walks into the kitchen.

What's all the hollering about?

Aunt Alice folds her arms across her chest and says, Jalmer, your mother here wants to care for the baby. She doesn't think May's doing a good job looking after her.

Pappa sighs.

167

You know I'm right Jalmer, Grandmother
Patience says. That child will meet her end by May
Amelia's neglect.

She's my sister! I say. I know Grandmother
Patience is so wrong. I'd never do anything to
hurt Baby Amy.

You are the most irresponsible child in this valley! Grandmother Patience shouts.

Mother! Pappa says. May Amelia's doing a fine
job with the baby and it's what Alma wants. As soon
as Alma's better, she'll take care of the baby herself.

But— Grandmother Patience says.

Enough Mother! This is the last I want to hear
of it.

I cannot believe Pappa has stuck up for me, a
no-good girl. I meet Pappa's eyes across the room
and smile with real thanks. He nods curtly and
leaves.

That night Baby Amy and I wake up to a real
racket.

Everybody in the house is sleeping when
Wilbert says to me Wake Up May I hear something
by the barn. Go get Pappa and wake him up.

But before I can even get out of bed and fetch
Pappa, there is a horrible roar and then all our

cows are mooing. Wilbert jumps up and grabs his gun and says You stay right here, May Amelia, you understand? Tell the boys to get to the barn quick.

I'm coming! I say.

You gotta stay with the baby, he says, and runs out of the room.

I stand in the kitchen and look out the window and cannot believe my eyes.

There is a big black bear in our barn and it has our old milking cow Liz in his jaws and is dragging her out. I learned how to be a real good milker on Old Liz. She's lame and can't stand on her leg to kick out, so she's a safe one to milk. She went lame on account of breaking her leg running when she heard the steamboat whistle late one night. She got scared and started to run across the field and fell in a hole. And now this mean old bear is trying to eat her up.

Old Liz is struggling, trying to get away from the bear but she can't on account of her lame leg.

All my brothers fire their guns in the air but don't get too close 'cause everybody knows that bears are real mean especially when they're hungry which this one surely is if it is bold enough to break into our barn. I wonder if it is the same bear that chased me up the tree.

169

The boys fire again, and the big bear growls and stands on its hind feet and it is real big, I cannot tell you how big, bigger than anything I have ever seen, and then Pappa goes running out of the house in his britches and takes aim and shoots the bear in the paw. The bear roars 'cause Pappa hit it, he's a real good shot, and then it drops down on all fours and runs off into the night.

Pappa comes in and sees me and Amy in the kitchen.

You gotta watch out for wild animals, May Amelia, gotta mind the baby, Pappa says. You saw how that bear killed Old Liz?

She's dead? I say.

Yeah, Wilbert says, that bear nearabout ripped off her head.

Pappa and Isaiah must now mend the barn with latches on the door so that no bear can get our cows again.

Baby Amy wakes up after everybody is back in bed. She is coughing something fierce, coughing like she can't catch her breath. Wilbert is sound asleep, snoring away. I slip out of the bed and light a candle.

Amy has rolled onto her belly and she is coughing away and when she sees me bending over the cradle she gives a wheeze. I pick her up and pat her on the back and she gurgles and her breathing becomes slow and steady.

I think of the bear getting near Baby Amy and it gives me a real chill. I hug her tight to my chest and she snuffles a little and looks up at me, blinking. It's just me and her in the light of the flickering candle.

Don't worry Amy Alice, I'll take good care of you. After all, you're the only Amy we've got.

CHAPTER NINE

~~

What Happened
on the Smith Island

Wilbert says I am grief crazy sad and the only way
to get rid of the sadness is to sleep it away.

But I know that this sadness will never go
away, it will tug me down with it into the box with
the lavender velvet wedding dress and I don't care
none at all because that is where I want to be, far
away from anything that remembers me, remembers my name is May Amelia Jackson, the sister of
Amy Alice Jackson, and for now even my very own
hands remind me of it all.

I know everyone is worried about me, even
Pappa, but I cannot help feeling this way. I want
to disappear so bad, sink into the woods where
no one can ever find me, not even the Indians, and
I am not afraid at all of going away if they would
only just leave me on the Baby Island that is all I

would want, to be left on the Baby Island in
the Nasel so that I can hear the leaves falling on
the water and the crickets chirping and know the
passings of the times. That is all I would want and
it is not so very much.

Wilbert is right I am grief mad but this hurt is
so deep I did not think that I had a place inside
me for it. I can't eat or sleep, it keeps calling on
and on, never stopping, like Grandmother Patience
and her nagging and scolding. I know it will never
change, it will never stop, like her gnarled cane,
evil and bent the way it is and leaving dark-blue
bruises and blood everywhere.

This is what happened.

I loved little Baby Amy like she was my baby,
and truth be told she *was* my baby, Mamma so
sick and all.

She looked at me like I was her ma, she slept
when I sang to her, smiled when I fed her from
the milk teat, our poor mamma too sick to feed
her. She looked fine, real pretty in the blanket
I made for her and even though it was cold and
bitter being winter and all, Wilbert found three
snowflowers and put them on the dresser. Ivan
and Alvin and Isaiah made her a cradle and I

put it right next to me and Wilbert's bed so I could be near her at night when she woke hungry and I had to feed her the milk. She was the most beautiful baby, everyone said she was so sweet-natured; even Kaarlo said so. At night I would wake up sometimes and just look at her sleeping in her cradle in the fine dress Wendell made her, like a real live angel come down from heaven.

Mamma was feeling better by and by but I still was the baby's mamma, caring and feeding and changing her and all. Wilbert helped me sometimes, although most the time he was afraid of dropping the little baby and I had to say Look Wilbert just hold the back of her head up like this. You got to hold up the back of the baby's head, they're real tender there.

Christmas Eve morning I woke up all excited on account of Joulupukki, St. Nicholas, coming to visit us children and bring us gifts. I was feeling like a new-minted penny all fresh and fine 'cause Baby Amy hadn't cried once all night. Come on little button I said, time to get up and eat, and so I picked her up but something was wrong, she was all stuck to the corner of the cradle, hard-like and cold, oh so cold and when

I put my ear to her heart I couldn't hear nothing, not the little pitter-pat, not the whispery breaths, nothing, and I started screaming Wilbert Wilbert Wilbert and everybody came running Isaiah Alvin Ivan Pappa Wendell and Kaarlo too but I kept screaming Wilbert Wilbert Wilbert and finally he came in from the barn I guess and said May what's the matter and I screamed so loud my very voice broke, even God could hear me I swear, the words clear from my mouth to the angels in heaven.

I said My Baby's Dead.

I cannot remember ever in my life being colder than on the day we buried Baby Amy in the grave-yard out on the Smith Island across from the schoolhouse, where my Uncle Henry first home-steaded years ago, high on the hill overlooking the Nasel.

Even the birds refused to chirp. Wilbert said it was too cold for the birds but I know it was because Baby Amy was dead and God tells every living thing when babies die and they mourn with us people.

No preacher told me this but I know it is the truth.

We put Amy in the dress Wendell had made her—it was real fine, so pretty-looking—and Mamma used her lavender velvet wedding dress to line the little casket Isaiah made. The box was a small one, much smaller than Nora's, and I thought the velvet would keep Baby Amy warm. There were no flowers to put on the grave, it being winter, only tired geraniums.

Everyone came from all around to the Smith Island for the burying. Wilbert said it was on account of Mamma having helped birth all the babes in the valley. Our poor sick mamma with the faraway look in her eyes who kept saying that Amy was the Loveliest Baby of them all.

Grandmother Patience came to the Smith Island too, and after the preacher finished his piece and it was silent enough to hear clear across the Nasel she said Poor Baby Amy, too bad her mamma never got to care for her and only May Amelia. She might well be alive today and not lying there beneath a pile of geraniums if May Amelia hadn't dealt with her.

Pappa's mouth dropped open and Mamma went all pale and all the boys looked at her with wide shocked eyes.

Wilbert said, That's a terrible thing to say Grandmother, there ain't a lick of truth to it.

It's true as my name is Patience Jackson, she said, the babe would be alive if this evil girl of yours hadn't handled her so.

And that is when I ran.

I ran so fast that Wilbert could barely catch up with me, ran and ran all the way to the Nasel—tossing off my coat it made me so slow—I ran ran ran to the little boat tied to the riverbank and jumped in with Wilbert shouting May May wait for me, don't go out by yourself, May May, come on May. But I couldn't hear him, I was far away already, far away from everything, so deep in my own memories of playing with Baby Amy that I barely knew I was in the middle of the Nasel in the little boat.

When Wilbert reached the bank he took another boat off the tie-up, I don't know whose boat, and paddled after me yelling and hollering May May come back stop and then he caught up, pulling his boat aside of mine and jumped in but I couldn't see him all I could see was Baby Amy wrapped in Mamma's wedding dress, the lavender velvet faded and so worn already, only threads in places, moth-eaten too, and I was wondering if she would be warm enough with only that tired old dress to keep her warm what with the sharp wind blowing off the Nasel and Wilbert started slapping me, slapping me hard saying May May come back May she's a wicked old woman May it wasn't your fault Baby Amy died because she just did babies die like that sometimes it's not your fault.

I had not cried, not one tear since Baby Amy had died and then all of a sudden I couldn't stop them, I cried and cried into Wilbert's neck. I cried and cried till my throat was sore and hurt so bad and I said Wilbert I ain't never going back there, take me away. Take me away.

And he did.

He brought me here to Uncle Henry and Aunt Feenie's house in Astoria. They had not come to the funeral on account of not getting the bad news in time. I cannot remember how we got there, only that I was cold through to my very bones, cold as the ground where Baby Amy lay. Wilbert says he thought he'd lost me, that he'd watched the light go out of my eyes when the horrible words left Grandmother Patience's mouth.

179

Somehow Wilbert convinced a gillnetter to take us across the Columbia in his bateau, the tide against us, the river so full of ice and the wind blowing so hard that he could barely see. Later they told us that it was a miracle we even made it across.

I imagine we must have been quite a sight on that cold winter day, us two children showing up in the dark, half frozen to death, me wearing Wilbert's coat having thrown mine off me and he frozen straight through from not having his coat to wear seeing as it was supposed to be warming me but not doing a very good job of it at all.

Uncle Henry answered the door when Wilbert knocked and he didn't blink twice to see two frozen children standing on his porch as if they had a right to be there, I swear I do not think anything shocks my uncle. He just said Feenie I believe we have got some children here for supper, best set out the extra plates.

Aunt Feenie came to the door, took one look at me and Wilbert, what a sight we must have made, and said Dear Lord children what on earth has happened?

And then I guess I fainted.

180

When I woke up I thought: *I am in heaven.* It was so warm and there was such a beautiful sweet voice talking to me, I was certain I was in paradise after all, but when I opened my eyes I saw that it was Aunt Feenie and I was in the most glorious bed, and she was bathing me off with warm water and rose soap and she said, Child don't you try to speak to me now you just rest, just close your eyes and rest and after a time I did just that.

The second time I woke up I heard someone screaming as if they had been killed or worse and I said to myself, Who is that poor soul screaming like that, as if their skin is being ripped off or something horrible I cannot imagine what and then all of a sudden I was being shook and I heard Wilbert saying Wake Up May Wake Up May and I realized it was me who was screaming. It was me.

After that Wilbert spent the night with me, burying us both beneath a nest of quilts, holding me tight, rocking me as if I was Baby Amy and saying over and over, May Amelia Jackson don't you give up on me, you hear me May, I am not about to stand for it, you come back to yourself

181

and me, do you understand me?

And then he rubbed my back, rubbed it warm and soft like he used to when we were small children and learning our alphabets, wrote my name on my back, a long swirly cursive M, a floppy A, a show-off hook of a Y.

And finally after a very long time I said I did not kill Baby Amy I did not she just fell asleep and didn't wake up, I didn't kill her Wilbert.

He just said I Know May.

I know.

I'm not going back, I say.

It is the first time I have spoken to Aunt Feenie since us children showed up on their porch.

Uncle Henry and Aunt Feenie exchange a glance. Wilbert has told them what happened on the Smith Island.

But May, Aunt Feenie says in a gentle voice. My kind gentle aunt.

I'm not, I say.

And that's that.

Pappa shows up on the porch and Aunt Feenie answers the door when he knocks.

We have been here one week.

He says, Morning Feenie, I come for my children.

Pappa doesn't look so good. He is real pale and looks older than I ever remember him but maybe that is just because I feel so old now myself. I remember Pappa saying he hoped that Mamma didn't have another girl, on account of me.

I knew no good would come of Mother living with you Jalmer, Aunt Feenie says, shaking her head. The child doesn't want to go with you. She wants to stay here. I discussed it with Henry and we'll be happy to keep her on for a spell.

Feenie, I don't think Alma's gonna be none too pleased about this, Pappa says.

Aunt Feenie puts her hand on my shoulder and says, The girl needs to mend. Let her stay Jalmer.

Wilbert says it must have been the shine to my eyes that made Pappa give in so easily. He says I had the look of the young widows of drowned gillnetters.

Pappa doesn't say anything; he just stares at me like he doesn't know what to do with a good-for-nothing girl like me. Finally he says, Well if that's what you want May Amelia. Come on Wilbert we've got work waiting for us on the farm.

Wilbert looks at me and says, Please Pa I'd like to stay here with May and look after her. She'll be so lonesome without me. Let me stay.

Pappa sighs real heavy, as if his own heart is breaking or something and I don't know, maybe it is. I never knew how to figure Pappa none too good. He just looks between Wilbert and me and says, Well fine then. You keep an eye on May Amelia for me and your ma.

Then Pappa turns to my uncle and says, Henry, I'd be much obliged if you could find my boy here some work in town so he can earn his keep.

He can help on my ship, Uncle Henry says, we're short a hand.

Thank you kindly Henry. I'll have Ivan and Alvin bring up your things, children, Pappa says. Be sure and come home and see your Mamma by and by, she'll be missing you but I suspect your Aunt Feenie is right and it won't do any harm for you to ride out the winter here.

He leans forward as if to give me a hug but I back away, until I am pressed up against Aunt Feenie's skirt. He sighs sadly and gives me and

184

Wilbert a pat on the head and walks back downhill to the docks.

I say, Wilbert, I will never go home. I will never forget what happened on the Smith Island.

Never.

CHAPTER TEN

‿ᴖᴗ

The Things I Have Seen

The things I have seen since I have been in Astoria could fill a book or a dream.

Every morning me and Wilbert go exploring all over town, looking for adventures. We take short-cuts through back alleys and all. Keep an eye out for smugglers and no-good Chinamen shang-haiers Uncle Henry always says. The smugglers and shanghaiers are exactly the reason we go looking and exploring around Astoria, 'cause there are smuggler dens everywhere—it's just a question of finding them and finding their treasure. Black Jake the Negro Sailor is rumored to have hidden out in a den somewhere in the basement hide-aways of Astoria's taverns.

Uncle Henry says that Astoria has the most saloons and taverns of any town in Oregon, that it is the most decadent town between San Francisco and Seattle. There are honky-tonk theaters and scandalous dance halls, and Wilbert tells me that you can pay with a salmon to get into them to see a show if you have no money.

There are lots of taverns in town and three of them set on the same row near the docks. All the boys who work the docks go and sit a spell in them after they get off the boats. It's where the gillnetters' and oystermen's wives go to find them. Uncle Henry says it's a darn-fool thing to spend time drinking with stinking sailors when you have a woman waiting at home for you.

There are not so many women here in Astoria, not even many Chinook women. Some of the boys send advertisements back east, to Boston and Nova Scotia too, 'cause there's plenty of Finns up that way. They write things like: "Bride wanted on frontier. Will pay for travel. Send picture." Aunt Feenie says the poor men are desperate for a good woman to look after them, and who can blame them? Wilbert tells me that Astoria is filled with nothing but hopeful bachelors.

Wilbert works on Uncle Henry's ship only a few days a week, so he has plenty of time to spend with me. I love living with Uncle Henry and Aunt

Feenie here in Astoria. Aunt Feenie's cookie jar is always full. And for once I don't have to worry about a herd of brothers, and disappointing everyone because I am a no-good girl always getting into trouble.

It is only Wilbert and me and it is just fine.

In the afternoons we go down to the docks and get fritters from Mariah's Tavern.

Sometimes I'll help out in the kitchen with the cooking when Mariah's short a hand, just cutting up vegetables and whatnot. She's a good cook, Mariah. Uncle Henry buys her all sorts of spices on his voyages, and so when she gets to cooking, things have a lot of flavor. She can cook oysters twelve different ways: fried, baked, fricasseed, poached, stew, soup, pies, you name it. I get a mite sick of all the oysters after I've worked with her. But the corn fritters are so very good, all hot and fresh and greasy. Why just thinking about them makes me hungry.

She gives Wilbert and me a basket and we set in the big hot kitchen to eat. Mariah's white hair is in its long slender braid with a red ribbon and looks real pretty. I don't think she looks scandalous at all.

189

Do you keep your money on your leg? Wilbert asks. 'Cause that's what Everybody says.

Mariah kicks out her leg and gives it a good shake.

Hear any coins rattling? Mariah asks, jiggling her leg.

No, we surely do not.

Well then, I guess Everybody is wrong, she says.

I've had something on my mind for a long time.

Did you shanghai my brother Matti to the Orient? I say.

Mariah just shakes her head at me and laughs and says, Why Miss May, I've been on real good behavior these days, I don't fancy the law coming after me. I'm not in the shanghaiing business anymore.

Wilbert says, Well, you should give the sheriff some of these here fritters and he won't bother you none.

Mariah laughs and says, The sheriff does have a taste for my fritters.

A mangy dog smells the fritters and starts howling in hunger at the back door of the kitchen. Mariah walks over and tosses it a fritter.

Hush now puppy, she says.

Mariah's not a bit like any of the stories. She's always laughing and happy to help out someone who is down on his luck. And she's always feeding us children. I know that she was supposed to have killed her husband but now I think it is just a tall tale. Mariah couldn't have killed anybody.

What's it like being a widow? I say.

Being a widow has its advantages, May, what with not having to look after some man all the time and cook his meals and tend to his mending.

Yeah, I say. Since we've been with Uncle Henry I don't have to take care of the farm or mind my brothers or cook for all the boys every night or anything.

We've had similar experiences I think then. My husband's been gone ten years now.

I say, My sister's dead.

Yes, I heard your sister died. Henry told me. I'm terribly sorry.

Her name was Amy, I say. Amy Alice Jackson.

That's a lovely name.

I picked it out myself.

Well then, Mariah says, that's certainly something.

Mariah puts her elbow into the stirring.

But I don't miss her, I say.

You don't? says Mariah.

Not really. She was just a baby.

Oh, I see.

Wilbert doesn't say anything—he's too busy eating the fritters. He's got grease dripping down his chin.

You know, Mariah says casually, my husband's been dead for a long time but I still miss him.

You do?

Sure I do. He was a good man. I loved him.

I remember how sweet Baby Amy smelled and how she used to gurgle up at me.

I guess I sorta miss Amy, I say.

You know May, Mariah says, it's okay to miss someone you love after they're dead.

I won't go back home, I say.

Why is that?

Because Grandmother Patience says I'm the one who killed Baby Amy.

Well May, both you and I know what the real truth is, don't we?

I remember Baby Amy's soft silky hair and how she would blink up at me with her wide, trusting eyes. I shake my head 'cause I don't know any truth at all, only that Amy's dead and buried and in the cold ground.

Mariah says, And you know what, I'd bet anything that Amy knows too and that's all that counts.

But my heart feels so sad it nearabout breaks. Baby Amy is gone forever, and all because of me.

Without any warning at all, Ivan and Alvin come to visit. They've brought my things in a small trunk with leather straps.

Mamma's packed my warm winter sweater inside and Susannah. Lying next to Susannah is a new outfit that Wendell has sewn for her, a pirate suit.

Wilbert says, Susannah will look very fierce indeed in the pirate outfit.

I expect she will Wilbert, I say. She is a very fierce doll you know. And I'll braid her hair in the Chinook way and then she'll be even fiercer.

Are you gonna flatten her head like the Chinooks do May Amelia? I'll fix you up a plank board to tie to her head, Wilbert teases.

The Chinooks flatten the heads of their babies when they are small. They put the infant between two planks and then the baby's head grows all

193

pointy like. Uncle Henry said Old Man Weilin told him that only the royal Chinooks flatten the heads—that it's a mark of royalty. It seems mighty strange to me. I would never have let anyone try and flatten Baby Amy's head.

I say, But Uncle Henry doesn't the baby's head get all mushed up?

That may be May Amelia but they seem like mighty smart folks to me, I expect they wouldn't go mushing up their heads if there wasn't a darn good reason.

Ivan and Alvin stay the night and Aunt Feenie cooks a real good supper, all sorts of treats. It's odd indeed to see Ivan and Alvin setting here at the table with Wilbert and me and Uncle Henry and Aunt Feenie.

So how've you been May? Alvin says.

Me and Wilbert have been fine. Astoria's a real exciting place to live, I say. There's all sorts of things to see here.

There's things to see in Nasel, Ivan says.

Astoria's nothing like the farm, I say.

That's for sure, says Wilbert.

Do you miss Nasel? Alvin asks.

Is Mamma better? I say, changing the subject.

Yeah, says Ivan.

194

That's good.

Why don't you come home, May? Alvin says.

'Cause we like it here fine.

Don't you miss Mamma and Pappa? Ivan says.

No, I lie. Why is he nagging me?

Don't you even miss me and Ivan? Alvin says.

No, I lie again.

May! Wilbert says, and shakes his head.

Well I don't, I say. I don't miss anything. I got plenty of things to do right here in Astoria, plenty of folks to see. Why there's nothing to see in Nasel, nothing but cows and farms and logs and a herd of useless boys. I was never happy to be there.

Alvin grits his teeth and glares at me. He doesn't speak to me for the rest of the night.

And neither does Ivan.

After supper Uncle Henry brings us children into his study, opens a camphor wood chest decorated with carvings, and takes out his navigating maps and charts. He spreads them out on the table and shows us how he sailed around the world to China and around the Cape Horn and nearabout everywhere so far as I can see. Ivan and Alvin don't pay attention to Uncle Henry—they're too busy glowering at me.

Aunt Feenie comes in and laughs at us, saying, Henry are you telling these children tales or truths?

Ever the truth Feenie, he says, and goes and gives her a kiss on the forehead. I cannot remember Pappa kissing Mamma like that. When I think of Pappa, all I remember is a scowl.

You children listen to what your Uncle Henry says but only believe half of it. He is a teller of tall tales.

Now that is simply an exaggeration, a real slur Feenie, Uncle Henry says.

Aunt Feenie wags her finger at Henry and says, Now my fine Neal McNeil did you tell them how you carried me off when I was but a girl of sixteen?

And a bonny lass your aunt was children, full of fire. Why, I took one look at her and knew she was the one for me.

I tell you May Amelia, beware of men with silver tongues, Aunt Feenie says. This devil here swept me clear away from all my friends and family in Finland and brought me to the wilderness, left me to go crazy on the Smith Island. Knappton was the closest town and was full of only bachelors and vagabonds, not a woman to be found. I tell you I was the lonesomest person on earth, even when Henry was in port.

I am trying to ignore the twins. But those no-good brothers of mine are doing a pretty good job of staring me down.

But your aunt had a fine hand with knitting the gillnets, didn't you, dearling? Uncle Henry says. When I was out at sea, your sweet aunt here would take pity on the poor bachelor gillnetters and take in some of their nets to knit and mend, since they had no wives of their own. Those gillnetters worked hard. They would go out on a Sunday night, come back on a Wednesday morn, leave again in the evening, and not be back home till Saturday night.

Wilbert yawns widely.

All right Henry, enough of your tales, these children need to be in bed. Ivan and Alvin have got to be up early to catch the boat back to Knappton.

Ivan and Alvin don't even look at me, they don't even say good night.

When Wilbert and I are in bed, Wilbert says, Ivan and Alvin are pretty upset at you, May.

I suspect they are, I say. But I don't want to go home Wilbert.

Wilbert nods his head. He knows my heart.

But the next morning there is no boat to be caught back to Knappton. The temperature dropped and the Columbia has frozen up like a sheet of glass. Me and Wilbert go ice-skating for hours on end, skating around the big ships moored on the docks, frozen to the rails. The ice is thicker than a child's fist. It is quite a sight to see all the ships frozen in the water. Ivan and Alvin just sit and stare at us from the docks. They're only speaking to Wilbert now, not to me.

Ivan and Alvin are lucky indeed that they have relations to stay with in Astoria, because many of the homesteaders who had taken the boat into Astoria to get provisions are trapped and cannot get back home.

And worse, Uncle Henry says, trapped knowing that their kin might be getting very hungry.

After four days of solid ice, folks are getting plain on desperate it seems, what with worrying about their kin, and so Captain Jordon who runs one of the boats, the *Gleaner*, announces that the ice has thawed enough to make the trip to the various homesteads and that all those folks who want passage are to show up at the docks at dawn.

Alvin says, May don't you want to come home with us?

198

I had almost forgotten what his voice sounded like.

No, I say.

Alvin grits his teeth and stomps away.

August Olson, an old sailing mate of Uncle Henry's, comes to supper the night before the *Gleaner*'s leaving. August Olson was a captain in the Finnish Navy, and he has a mighty fierce look to him, a real black beard and bright-blue eyes and a big old scar on his cheek where the blade of a crosscut saw sliced it open during a bad storm.

That Captain Jordon is a greedy fool. Any seaman can tell there's a storm brewing, Uncle Henry says. What's the point of risking the lives of folks?

I have a mighty bad feeling about the *Gleaner*, Henry, Mr. Olson says.

I won't let these nephews of mine on that ship. There's a storm rolling in, believe me, Uncle Henry says nodding at Ivan and Alvin.

August Olson shakes his head and says, My only son Erik is set on going on it, even though I warned him not to. He's anxious to get home to his wife and new baby. That boat will never even make it to Knappton between the snags, ice floes, and coming storm, it's sailing straight to the devil and if I end up burying my son there'll be a killing,

199

because I, August Olson, will lynch Captain Jordon and fillet him like a salmon.

After supper Alvin, who is again not talking to me, says, We're going on that boat. We're not staying a minute longer.

You can't go, Wilbert says. You heard Uncle Henry, it's too dangerous.

I don't care, Alvin says, stubborn. You and May don't miss us none—you should be happy to see us go. You got so much to See Here In Astoria, he says.

Wilbert tries to convince them to stay, but no matter what he says, those twin brothers of ours don't listen. They're like dumb cows who won't come in during a snowstorm, who just stand there till they're dead from the cold.

They won't go, I say. They're just trying to scare us Wilbert.

I hope so May, he says.

Wilbert and me get up early the next morning intending to go down to the docks and get some breakfast at Mariah's. I'm lacing my shoes when I hear Wilbert.

Ivan and Alvin are gone! Wilbert shouts.

And sure enough, none of their things are in

the bedroom. They must have left very early indeed. I get a bad feeling in the pit of my belly, a feeling that says maybe I was wrong.

Wilbert says, Come on May, we gotta do something. We can't let them get on that boat.

As we run down the streets, my heart beats faster and faster, I think it will explode. It will be All My Fault if something happens to Ivan and Alvin and I cannot bear the thought of a world without them in it.

Hurry Wilbert! I say. I am praying for a real miracle.

Down at the docks there's a real big crowd, everyone's jostling to get on the *Gleaner*. But the twins are nowhere in sight.

Let's split up, Wilbert says.

I run around the crowd and try to push my way in but people just push me right on back.

We gotta find them, I say to myself.

And then, near the front of the line, I can see two shiny blond heads bobbing in the mess of people.

There they are, I holler to Wilbert, pushing through the crush.

Alvin has his ticket out and is handing it to a deckhand when I grab him by the arm.

Don't go, I say.

Why? Alvin says grimly, his face set.

It's real dangerous, Uncle Henry said so himself, I say.

Ivan glares at me. We're not scared of anything, he says.

Come on Ivan, Alvin says. Let's get on board.

I tug hard on Alvin's arm, I won't let him go.

Don't, I plead.

Why shouldn't we? Alvin says.

He has a hard look in his eyes, a look that is pure stubbornness. I know what I have to do.

'Cause I don't want to lose anyone else, not even a pair of stubborn brothers I've missed every day, I say.

Alvin just stares at me, like he's not expecting me to say that, to say that I've missed him and Ivan.

Well? I say.

Alvin smiles and snatches his ticket back and Ivan grabs me up and gives me a hug.

Don't get all mushy I say, but even still, I hug him back tight.

We walk home for breakfast. The *Gleaner* leaves and neither of my brothers is setting on its deck.

202

August Olson's terrible prediction comes true. The *Gleaner* was near Knappton when a sudden wind blew against the boat's broadside and capsized it. Nobody knows yet who has lived and who has died, only that the ferry is now on the bottom of the Columbia. But Ivan and Alvin, my stubborn twin brothers, are not on the river bottom with it.

The sight of them safe and sound in Uncle Henry and Aunt Feenie's house is the best thing I've seen here in Astoria.

CHAPTER ELEVEN

A Sorry Girl Indeed

Eventually the ice melts and Ivan and Alvin get back to the farm, but not before we have some fun together. I am sad that they leave, but not too sad because for the first time ever I have a friend who is a girl. Her name is Emma Saari. She is Finnish like me and has long blond hair, which her mother braids every morning. She's a Proper Young Lady.

Emma is my age, twelve years only, but sometimes she sounds all grown up, like Miss McEwing, especially when I tell her my dreams about wanting to have adventures and sail the world with Wilbert.

You've been playing with boys for too long May Amelia, she says. You're starting to think like one.

That may be. But it seems to me, I say, that it's the boys who get to do all the exciting things while the girls get left behind. I don't want to be left behind.

She is so much fun to be with, even though she says I Am A Sorry Girl. Emma says you're supposed to use your charm to get out of difficult situations. I told her about the time the bear chased me up the tree and said that the bear didn't care one bit indeed if I was charming or not. She said she could see my point.

I've noticed that Wilbert always looks especially clean when Emma is coming to play with us. I suspect that he likes her.

I tell this to Emma and she laughs, her high sweet laugh, and says, Wilbert? Why I like that Ed Grady, he's so tall and handsome, don't you think?

Ed Grady is a sailing hand on Uncle Henry's ship so Emma always wants to come along when Wilbert and I go to the shipyard. I don't know about that Ed Grady; I can't imagine ever actually liking a boy the way Emma does. Not Emma though.

How fine it will be when I get to kiss Ed, she says.

Emma closes her eyes and twirls around.

I say, Emma, you must be crazy as a lunatic if you're thinking of kissing a boy. I'd sooner kiss one of Isaiah's sheeps.

Emma says, May Amelia, I swear, don't you have any romantic notions in that head of yours?

I guess I don't.

I tell Emma everything—what it's like to live in Nasel and how I'm happy to be in Astoria, happy to be just another girl, not the only no-good girl around. Even though Wilbert is still my best friend, telling things to another girl feels good in a way I can't explain. She has a different way of looking at things.

My, Emma says, your pappa sounds very hard indeed, but it does seem like you get into a lot of mischief. If I did those things my father would whip me for sure. Your pappa just yells at you.

I hadn't ever thought of it like that.

And really, Emma says, it must be nice to have so many handsome brothers.

Handsome?

Handsome and charming, Emma says, like that Ed Grady.

But they're always teasing me.

What about your Aunt Alice? She sounds interesting.

You're sorta like Aunt Alice, I say.

Like how? she says, wrinkling her nose just like Aunt Alice.

All pretty like she is, and always wearing dresses and looking like a real Proper Young Lady.

That's what girls are *supposed* to do May Amelia. You're supposed to wear dresses and comb your hair. Didn't anyone ever tell you that?

Emma shakes her head, stray curls bobbing. She is wearing a fine white dress with lacy edging and it hasn't a mark on it. Mamma won't sew me white dresses on account of me climbing trees. I suspect Emma has never climbed a tree in her life.

I hate dresses, I say. You can't run or play or climb a tree in them.

May Amelia Jackson, Emma says, you are hopeless.

We go to see Aunt Alice. She is having her afternoon tea.

May Amelia, she says, how are you darling?

Hi Aunt Alice, this is Emma.

I am delighted to make your acquaintance Emma. My, what a lovely dress. May Amelia, we have *got* to get you into a dress like that one of these days. Would you girls like some tea?

Yes please, Emma says. She is so polite, she really is like a miniature Aunt Alice.

We are in the sitting room and Aunt Alice pours tea and passes around a plate of ginger cookies.

Now May, how is that mischievous brother of yours? Aunt Alice asks.

Which one? I say.

Aunt Alice laughs.

Emma, she says, did you know that my niece here has got herself seven brothers? And each and every one a real gentleman.

I sure don't know about that gentleman part. Emma is busy looking around Aunt Alice's fine house, admiring her pretty curtains and china.

I only got six now since Matti's been shanghaied, I say.

Your brother Matti shanghaied? What a lot of nonsense, Aunt Alice says.

It's true, I say. Uncle Aarno says he was drinking at Mariah's and got himself shanghaied. We haven't seen him since.

Aunt Alice shakes her head like I've got it all wrong.

May Amelia, your brother Matti has not been

shanghaied. He is living in San Francisco and
doing fine.

I don't understand.

Why, he married the O'Casey girl, she says.

The Irish girl? The one everyone thinks is
drowned?

They eloped, Aunt Alice says simply.

But how do you know? Uncle Aarno doesn't
even know what happened.

Because I helped them. I always was a softy for
romance, Aunt Alice says with a gleam in her eye.

I sit back and shake my head. I cannot believe
this. Aunt Alice? Why she never does anything
sneaky. She's a Proper Lady. I try to imagine Matti
with his Irish girl, imagine that they are happy, living in an exciting faraway place.

Does Mamma know? I ask.

Yes, I told her a little while back.

And Pappa?

No May, your pappa has no idea. No idea at all.
Why, he's the very reason they had to run away.

Because Mary's Irish?

Yes May Amelia, Aunt Alice says. You must
promise me that you will tell no one. This is a very
great secret just among us ladies and I don't think
your father would ever forgive me if he found out.

I don't think Pappa would either. I actually feel sorry for Pappa. His favorite son ran away because of him.

I suspect your brother Matti will write your folks and tell them the truth after a little time has passed, Aunt Alice says. Until then, we have to keep our lips sealed.

You can count on me, I say. I look at Emma and Aunt Alice, and it feels special that us three have a secret.

How daring, says Emma. I want to elope some-day.

Aunt Alice sits back and smiles at her.

Well, maybe when you're old enough I'll help you too.

Wilbert and I have made another new friend in Astoria and he is a Chinaman. Otto is only eleven, younger than me even, but he is ever so clever. He can speak Chinese and Finnish and English and some Chinook too, 'cause he learned it from some Chinook children. Otto's father is Joe Cheng, who is the foreman at the Seaborg Cannery here in Astoria and is responsible for all the Chinamen who work there.

All the Chinamen have to work in the cannery,

Otto says. They're not allowed to fish.

The men live in the China House but Otto and his parents have their own house next door. Otto knows near just about everybody in Astoria, and he knows all the good haunts on account of he's lived here so long. Otto wears pajama pants like the Chinamen I've seen down at the docks. It's hard to believe that we are friends with a real live Chinaman.

Today Otto runs up to us and says, Your Uncle Henry's down at the jail!

What? says Wilbert.

He's trying to get August Olson out!

Let's go! I say.

Otto leads the way through the streets to the Astoria jailhouse. There is a real crowd outside, and Uncle Henry is at the front of it Raising A Ruckus.

The sheriff is trying to calm Uncle Henry.

Look Henry, August just plain hunted down Captain Jordon and beat him till he couldn't move. I had to put him in the jail. I have to keep the peace, says the sheriff. The sheriff is a nice man, but he is the fourth sheriff Astoria has had this year. Not one seems to like the job very much. The fact that Astoria is the most lawless town around these parts might have something to do with it.

That Damn Jordon's the one who should be in jail, not August! Uncle Henry hollers, his red mustache twitching fiercely.

Calm down Henry, the sheriff says, holding up his hands beseechingly.

But Uncle Henry's all steamed up.

Jordon's the reason August's son is on the bottom of the Columbia, and all those other folks with him. You know he should never have taken the boat out! Uncle Henry shouts.

But Henry—

Let him out of that jail, do you hear me? That's an innocent man you got in there, that's not justice!

The crowd roars and the sheriff shakes his head sadly but goes on into the jail.

Your Uncle Henry's quite a fellow, says Otto.

That's for sure, says Wilbert.

A moment later the sheriff walks out, escorting August Olson who shakes his fist in the air. The crowd starts cheering.

To Mariah's! shouts Uncle Henry, wrapping an arm around August, and everybody heads down to the tavern.

Well I'll be, says Otto. They'd never let a Chinaman outta jail.

What do you mean? I say.

We're nothing but workers, May Amelia, nobody would ever stand up for us. Why they'd just ship us back to the Orient.

I wonder if Otto is maybe exaggerating, but his eyes are steady. I didn't know they could do that here, in America.

That's just terrible, I say.

Otto shrugs and says simply, But It's the Truth.

It gets me thinking. Maybe they'd ship me to Finland if I got into some real trouble because I'm a Finn. That sure would be exciting. It's one way to travel the world.

Emma and I visit Uncle Henry's ship on account of Emma wanting to spy on Ed Grady.

Uncle Henry's ship is a 168-foot-long, two-deck, three-masted bark called the *Coloma*. It has a carved figure of a mermaid at the head of it and carries lumber from Astoria all the way to the Orient. I've noticed that the mermaid's face bears a resemblance to Aunt Feenie's. Uncle Henry has a crew of twenty-five men when he goes out to sea, but when he is in port there are only five men on board.

Wilbert has been helping repair the rigging that got damaged in a storm the last time Uncle Henry was out to sea. He gets to climb the high masts and Ed Grady says that Wilbert moves faster than the monkeys he's seen climbing the trees in the jungles of Africa. Ed Grady has such wonderful stories from all his travels, and he has been nearabout everywhere. He is tall and his face is real brown from being out in the sun all the time. And he's real old, why, he is nearly thirty.

He says, Hello Emma, Hello May Amelia.

Hi Ed, Emma says with a big smile.

What are you lovely ladies up to today?

Just visiting Wilbert, I lie.

Must get back to work ladies, Ed says with a wink and walks away.

Wilbert comes up and says, Hi Emma.

But Emma only has eyes for Ed. She is watching him order some sailors about.

Emma, I say, Ed's too old for you.

But he's not married.

Why would you want to go and get married? I say.

Just because! she says, and stomps off, following Ed Grady like a puppy.

I sure do like Emma but I don't understand her one bit.

215

And now Emma is all excited because there is to be a dance on Friday and she is making a new dress to wear.

What will you wear May Amelia? she says.

I can't go. I'm too young, my ma and pa won't let me.

But Emma is real clever. She says, Well May Amelia, you aren't exactly living with your ma and pa now, are you? I suspect your Aunt Feenie would let you go.

I haven't got a thread to wear I say, eyeing my overalls.

Why don't we make a little visit to your Aunt Alice? She has a fine hand with sewing and if anyone has some extra fabric lying around, it's her.

Emma is clever for sure, and besides this is something only girls can do together. Even though I am not fond of dresses, Emma makes it sound real exciting, so maybe it is. We go over and visit Aunt Alice, who is real pleased to see me and my charming friend Emma.

Emma wastes no time in explaining the situation to her, and the next thing I know, I am standing on a stool in my drawers while the two of them tack calico fabric around me. I am so full of

216

pins that I can hardly breathe, let alone wiggle.
They leave me standing there like a porcupine
while they walk around me and adjust this hem
and that tuck and nip the waist in just a bit tighter
here and there. I can't take it anymore.

Get Me Outta These Darn Pins, I say.

Emma is right shocked at my language.

She says, May Amelia you curse like a boy. You
should mind your language—you'll never get a
fella if he hears you talking like that.

I say, I don't care about getting a fella, I got
seven brothers already, why would I need another
boy anyways?

They say I'd be happier if I was more like a
Proper Young Lady but I suspect they are the ones
that'd be happier, not me.

Aunt Alice and Emma just shake their heads
at me.

They both agree that I am A Sorry Girl Indeed.

Finally Friday comes, and not a moment too
soon.

I am so darn sick of pinning and poking and
trying on petticoats and discussing how to put a
ribbon in my hair that I don't care if I go to the
dance after all. They have got me stuffed into this

dress so tight I can barely sneeze. I thought a dance would be heaps more fun than this.

After Aunt Alice finishes fixing me in the dress, Wilbert and me go to Emma's house to fetch her. Wilbert's eyes just about fall out of his head when he sees her walking down the stairs in her fine yellow dress; she looks a picture to be sure.

Me and Wilbert and Emma get to the hall, but nobody's really dancing, just all the girls are setting on one side of the room looking like dressed-up dolls and all the boys are setting on the other side scratching at their stiff shirt collars.

I get a handful of cookies and set down in a corner to watch the proceedings. There's a lively fiddle player and soon enough folks get to dancing, but I can't be bothered. I swear, it's so boring being a Girl sometimes.

Some boy with big ears comes up to me and says, Do You Wanna Dance?

I am just plain shocked. I cannot imagine having to dance with this boy.

Thanks but I don't feel too well, I say, and run outside.

There is no way I'm going back inside. I decide to go and visit Otto.

I knock on the door to his house and his

mamma answers. She smiles at me and calls back into the room. Otto comes running to the door.

I thought you went to the dance, he says.

It was boring.

Otto nods. He's not much interested in dances either.

I have to do something. You want to come with me? he asks.

Sure, I say.

He leads me down to the bay. There is a full moon so it's easy to see the clear water.

What's going on? I say.

Look, Otto says, and he points his finger out at the water. A bateau is sailing toward where we are standing on the craggy rocks.

It's just a gillnetter, I say.

No, Otto says. They're smugglers.

Real live smugglers right here in Astoria? Smuggling what? Maybe treasure, maybe gold ingots, maybe silk from the Orient?

What're they smuggling, I say. Gold?

People, he says.

What do you mean? Like shanghaied slaves or something?

No, no. That gillnetter works for the Seaborg Cannery and they need more workers and so they send for Chinamen from the Orient, but they can't bring them during the day 'cause it's illegal on account of them not having proper papers, so they smuggle them here at night and I bring them over to the factory.

Why don't they have papers? I say.

It takes too long to get them.

But won't they get caught?

Otto rolls his eyes and says, Nobody can seem to tell any Chinamen apart—they think we all look alike, so how can you get caught?

Otto surely does have a point.

The smuggling bateau pulls up to the beach and Otto steps out with a lantern and about six Chinamen get out and walk over to us. Otto gestures to them and says something in Chinese and then we're off, running through the tideland weeds, staying low, all the way to the China House. When we get to the China House, an old Chinese woman lets us in through a basement. There is a big table set with all sorts of food in bowls and it smells awful good.

Me and Otto have a little midnight snack with the new Chinamen. I speak Finnish with Otto and Otto speaks Chinese with the Chinamen. It's a very confusing night indeed, everyone's laughing and chattering—why it's like a real party. And Otto's mamma is just like my own mamma, the way she is wearing a big apron and dishing out food to everybody and scolding Otto when he forgets his table manners; it's just like a normal family even though they are all Chinamen. I don't see what Otto meant about people looking the same. They all look different to me. Why, one of them's got a real skinny face, and the fella sitting across from me has round cheeks that look like apples.

The food is real tasty too, all sorts of soups with seaweed and salmon and these things that Otto says are called noodles, it's not at all like what the Finns cook. It's much nicer than fish-head stew. I wouldn't mind living here one bit.

This is heaps more fun than that stuffy old dance, I say.

That's for sure, says Otto. You're not very good at being a girl.

That's what Emma says too. She says I am A Sorry Girl.

She's right but you sure are heaps more fun than a real girl, he says.

I suspect that I should Take Offense but by his grin I know he intends it to be a compliment.

221

I am having a hard time using the sticks to pick up the food. Otto says that they're called chopsticks and they're very tricky indeed. More of the food is ending up on my dress than in my belly. Finally Otto says something to his mamma and she brings me over a big spoon.

By the time I'm ready to go home I have a full stomach.

Thank you kindly, I say, and start walking down the quiet street. When I look back, Otto and his kind mamma with the big smile are standing in the door, her hand on his shoulder.

And for a moment I miss my very own mamma so much it hurts.

Aunt Feenie is waiting on the porch for me. She eyes my dress which has got mud on it from mucking about and food all down the front. She smiles wryly and says, You look real pretty in that dress, did you have a nice time at the dance dear?

I guess she's just happy that I'm in a proper dress for a change. I say, I had a real fine time.

She says, Where is your brother Wilbert?

I say I don't rightly know, but I suspect that he is with Emma.

Wilbert gets home real late and he is one big

smile, even his eyes are sparkling, so I say, Did you catch a kiss from Emma?

And he says, May Amelia, gentlemen don't talk of such things.

I say, Wilbert, you're surely no gentleman.

But he wouldn't say a word so I suspect that he did get a kiss after all.

CHAPTER TWELVE

A Lucky Doll

It is the first day of March when Pappa appears on the front porch of Aunt Feenie and Uncle Henry's house.

Aunt Feenie says, Your Grandmother Patience has died God rest her soul, and we must go to Nasel for the funeral. I expect your mother will want you and Wilbert back with her, so pack up your trunk and we'll take it when we go.

Me and Wilbert look at each other. Grandmother Patience is dead? I cannot believe my ears.

How'd she die? Wilbert says.

The scarlet fever's come to the valley and many folks are real sick, Pappa says. Pappa doesn't look too good himself. He's thinner than I remember.

Pappa shakes his head and says, Your brother Wendell has been sick nigh on three weeks and your poor mother is plumb worn out between nursing him and every other soul who comes to our door in the middle of the night for her medicines. It's real bad May Amelia, and I'm of a mind not to bring you children home and risk you getting sick too but we're drowning and your ma needs another hand to help her.

Wilbert says, Has anybody else died?

Well, so far your Grandmother Patience and Lonny's ma, Mrs. Petersen, are the only ones. They have closed the schoolhouse, as they don't want the sick children infecting the healthy ones. Now get on and pack your things, time's a-wasting.

I truly thought I would never want to see the Nasel or our homestead again. But as we row up the Nasel, the familiar sight of our house nestled in the valley with the great mountains rising around it makes my heart beat faster.

All the boys are waiting to see me—Alvin, Ivan, Kaarlo, and even Isaiah, who has left the sheeps to come and welcome me and Wilbert back. I look around.

Where's Wendell? I say.

Mamma looks worn out, but she is real glad to see me and Wilbert. He's sick in bed, she says.

Bosie comes charging in, yipping and barking at me. He jumps all over me and nearabout
knocks me down. I guess he missed me too.

Get Down Bosie, I say.

Me and Mamma, we sit in the kitchen at the
table. Everything is the same, even the smells.
Mamma tells me everything that has passed since
we've been gone, how she worried after us and
was sad as a mother could be about losing Amy
but that God Works In Strange Ways and that she
was a lucky woman to have only lost one of her
children when so many folks lose all theirs and my
what a shame it was that Grandmother Patience
was called to God, but she'd had a full life, she
was an old woman and there's no reason to cry
when an old person passes on, it's the way it's supposed to be.

I say I'm not sad Mamma, Grandmother hated
me.

And Mamma, why, she just reaches over and
pulls me tight against her faded gunnysack dress,
all smelling of flour, and gives me a squeeze.

She says, I'm not sad either May Amelia. Your
Grandmother Patience hated nearabout every living thing.

I stay home with Wendell while everyone else goes to Grandmother Patience's funeral. Wendell is pretty weak and has a real sore throat and he spends a lot of time complaining and saying May Can You Bring Me Some Soup, and May Can You Bring Me Some Water, and May Can You Bring Me Some Bread.

Now I know that Mamma is a strong woman if she can put up with nonsense like this all the time.

Wendell says that he is happy that I'm back, that Bosie has not barked once since we left and that the kittens were crying for me all the time.

I brought back Susannah, I say.

Wendell coughs and gives me a weak smile.

I'm glad, he says, I missed Susannah too.

All the folks who attend the funeral come back around to our house afterward and bring all sorts of nice food. There's cobbler, roast duck, venison stew, squeaky cheese, and my very favorite, fresh *pulla*, which is Finnish bread flavored with cardamom topped with sugar icing. Uncle Aarno has even brought his last bit of smoked salmon.

They said a service for Grandmother in the Rukoushuone. Wilbert tells me that Grandmother Patience needs all the prayers she can get and he doubts she's in heaven, on account of her meanness.

Just about everybody in the valley has come to our house and it seems more like a party than a funeral, what with the men drinking and singing old Finnish sailing tunes and the women all gossiping in the kitchen about this and that. I am kept very busy indeed, making sure that there is plenty of food on the table and that Wendell is comfortable in his sickbed. Pappa has banished Bosie and Buttons to the barn, but there are quite a few children here, and Wilbert is talking with Lonny.

Lonny I'm real sorry to hear about your mamma dying like she did, I say, but Lonny just shakes his head.

Wilbert says, Let's steal a pie and go to the barn and play with Bosie, just us three.

I take a mince pie made of venison and apples and raisins and we sneak out the back and run into the barn. It's all snug and warm and cozy, and we climb up the ladder to the hayloft and Wilbert spreads a horse blanket down on the hay and we sit there and eat the mince. Buttons sidles up and mews for a scrap.

Lonny's a big boy, and he goes at the mince pie like he hasn't eaten in years. Between mouthfuls

Lonny explains how quickly his ma died, how he still expects to hear her hollering for him to fetch some wood, or build up the fire, but that she's well and truly dead, and that our brother Isaiah went over and built the box for her 'cause his pa was too drowned in the bottle to so much as lift a hammer.

He seems so calm about it all that I cannot help myself.

I say, Do you miss her Lonny? Do you miss your ma?

And he has just taken a bite of mince and then his face sort of screws up and he spits out the mince onto the hay and starts crying, bawling great big tears, and Wilbert and I put our arms around him and hug him tight, let him cry into my apron until it is soaked clear through.

Why isn't she coming back? he wails. Why can't I go to heaven and visit her? I miss my ma!

Shhh, I say, it's gonna be all right. And my eyes meet Wilbert's.

You've got Wilbert and me, I say. You still got us.

I get no sleep at all, between thinking about Lonny's ma and nursing Wendell. It is the first

time I have been back in me and Wilbert's bedroom since Baby Amy died. Somebody has taken
away the cradle; it is nowhere in sight. And for no
reason at all that I can figure, I keep thinking of
Amy, waiting to hear her wake up and cry, across
the room.

Wendell is up all night, feverish. I stay up with
him, as Mamma is just too tired after nursing
Grandmother into the grave. Poor Wendell mutters
a lot about Wild Cat Clark and Susannah and I
cannot understand what all. He is burning up but
keeps saying that he's freezing, which makes no
sense. I cool him off with water from the Nasel that
Wilbert fetches for me. All the boys lend a hand.
Ivan and Alvin set by the stove and keep an eye on
the broth that's simmering there and Isaiah helps
build up the fire. I can tell that even Kaarlo is worried by the way he keeps sticking his head in the
door and asking if Wendell's any better.

Wilbert comes in and sits with me for a time.

I say, Do you think Wendell's gonna die like
Lonny's ma?

Wilbert looks at me real shocked like, sur-
prised that I would suggest such a thing, and says,
There Is No Way Wendell Is Going To Die Do You
Understand Me, May Amelia?

231

I say, Yes I understand you, Wilbert, I am not an idiot; I am not slow like Lonny.

Well then May, why did you ask such a foolish question? Do you want to put the hex on him with your talk?

For the first time ever I think that Wilbert does not understand me, so I try to explain.

But Wilbert, Baby Amy died and now Wendell could too. You know he could! We've got the bad Jackson luck again.

The bad luck's not back! he shouts.

I think Wilbert is scared of Wendell dying.

And he doesn't understand that I'm scared too.

The next morning Wendell is still very bad. He is burning up, his skin is hot to touch, and nothing will bring down the fever, not even Mamma's willowbark tea. He's throwing up, he can't keep anything in his stomach, not even water. And he's covered with red bumps everywhere. A scarlet rash.

When Mamma sees the red bumps, she starts crying. It is a bad sign.

I can't bear to lose another child Jalmer, she says, weeping into my father's chest.

When I hear that, I am so angry I cannot say a word. I just grab Wilbert and run out of the house.

We hafta do something! I shout. We can't just let Wendell die!

Wilbert shakes his head. He is stuck. We have never known our mamma to give up like this. I think hard. Bosie has followed us out into the yard and nips at my leg. He wags his tail and gives a yelp.

What about Chinook medicine? I say.

Yeah! says Wilbert.

After all, Jane mended Bosie.

Let's go! I tell Wilbert, and we run down the front path.

Wait, I say, and run back inside for Susannah.

We need all the help we can get.

Old Man Weilin and Wild Cat Clark are setting on the porch smoking pipes when we come running up.

What do you rapscallions want? Old Man Weilin says, blowing smoke out in rings.

Wendell's sick! He's got the fever, I say. We need to get some medicine.

Bad luck, Wild Cat says.

The Old Man nods his head. Go on around back, he says. That wife of mine should have some tonic.

We knock on the door to the cedar house and Jane opens it.

Wendell's sick and Mamma thinks he's gonna die! I say. He's got the fever and we have to save him!

Jane nods her head and disappears into a back room. She returns carrying a small jar.

It's Yiu-yu sweat, she says, Very good for fever.

Thanks, Wilbert says, taking the jar from Jane and tucking it into his shirt.

I see you brought Susannah, Jane says. There's something I've been meaning to give you.

Jane has made Susannah a Chinook dress just like hers. It is made of young cedar bark that has been beaten soft and then woven into a long tunic with a fringe. Susannah looks like a real Indian princess.

She looks fine, I say.

We gotta go, says Wilbert.

We are almost out the door of the lodge when Jane says, Wait.

Jane sticks a long black feather inside Susannah's dress.

From Ta-mah'na-wis, the Guardian Spirit. For good luck, she says, and smiles.

Wendell is still tossing and turning when we get home; his skin is hot to the touch. Mamma gives him Jane's tonic and says Cross Your Fingers Children.

I put Susannah on the table next to Wendell's bed and sit in the rocking chair, the same chair I rocked Baby Amy in. I mop his head with a wet cloth. His skin is still red and bumpy like fleas have been at him. But I know the bumps aren't from fleas, but from the fever.

Please don't die, Wendell, I can't lose you too.

When I wake up, Bosie is licking my hand and my neck has a crick in it on account of me falling asleep in the rocking chair.

Stop It Bosie, I say grumpily.

I hear a sigh and look over at the bed. Wendell is squinting at me in the early-morning light. His glasses are on the table next to the bed. He reaches a hand out and slides them on.

That's a fine dress Susannah has on her May, Wendell says weakly.

I put my hand on his head and it's cool as can be.

Yes, I say. Jane made it for her, for luck.

Wendell smiles.

Susannah is a lucky doll indeed.

CHAPTER THIRTEEN

Happy to Be Here

It is finally spring, but I am feeling sad even though the yellow daffodils are pushing their heads out of the ground and the crocuses too. Now that Wendell is better and I have time to think, it seems that every little thing reminds me of Baby Amy and not even Buttons the cat or Bosie and his tricks can cheer me up.

I'm feeling low, I say.

Wilbert says, I bet Lonny's feeling a whole lot worse than you May, alone in that house like he is with no mamma. Let's go and visit him.

Lonny is just setting on his porch mending an old net of his pa's when we walk up. He looks sort of mangy, like his clothes haven't been washed in a long time and there is a long streak of dirt on his cheek. His face lights up when he sees us.

Hiya Lonny, Wilbert says.

I peek inside the front door of his house. It's a real mess. It looks as if a woman has not been in this house for the whole winter. I don't ask Lonny where his pa is because from what Kaarlo heard, it seems that Mr. Petersen has taken to working at the lime quarry out near Knappton. Lonny's left by himself all day from what anyone can tell, doesn't go to the schoolhouse anymore since his ma's not there to tell him to and has nearabout forgotten any of the English that he learned.

I tug Wilbert aside. Wilbert, I say, we gotta clean this place, it's not fit for Bosie in the state it's in now. Lonny can't do it on his own and his pa's sure not been paying it any mind.

Wilbert and I set about helping Lonny clean his house. It smells awful bad and there is washing needing to be done everywhere. I send Wilbert and Lonny off to our house to fetch some lye. I sort things out, put all the washing to be done in a big basket by the door, open the windows to air out the rooms, and scrub the floors downstairs. After I have done the upstairs I will polish all the floors with skim milk so that they have a shine.

In the kitchen there is no food, just baskets

238

of old rotting vegetables, mostly tideland grasses from the looks of it. I suspect that Lonny has not had a proper meal since his ma died and probably has been eating only goosetown greens, which are stewed tideland grass roots. They are nasty tasting.

When the boys get back, I send them out to fetch fresh hay from the barn for the mattress ticks and to pick daffodils although Wilbert puts up a bit of a fuss about having to pick flowers.

You can always do the washing, I say, setting a big copper pot to boil on the stove. He thinks better of it and grabs Lonny's hand and leaves. I put the cotton sheets in the boiling water and hope they come out looking better than they did going in.

I clean the house slowly, room by room, and have the boys take out the old hay, which is full of bugs and the Lord knows what else.

When I get to Lonny's ma and pa's bedroom I stop and wonder if I should go in, then decide that it probably needs to be cleaned. But it's clean as a whistle, the cleanest room in the house. There is truly not a speck of dirt in the room, not a cobweb, nothing. Maybe Lonny's ma is haunting this room, coming back and cleaning it herself. It's a very nice room, actually, with a fine pine sleighbed and a big wardrobe and a small ladylike dresser, which I suspect was hers.

I imagine Mrs. Petersen, with her wide hips and white hair, smoothing the top of the dresser clean with the hem of her apron, the same apron she used to wipe the corner of Lonny's mouth when he was a baby. Whenever I think of her, I picture her in that same white starched apron and I wonder if they buried her in it or if maybe Lonny's pa simply burned it in the fireplace, burned it away so he wouldn't be reminded of how soft her cheeks were and how she never got the hang of speaking English.

After I look through all the cupboards in the kitchen, it's clear that there's not a bite of food in the house, so I decide to invite Lonny and his pa over for supper.

Supper is a festive occasion, and I for one am a sorry child indeed that not one of us thought to invite Lonny and his pa over sooner. Mr. Petersen is just bursting with things to say, he's practically babbling and he devours every bite of food that's put in front of him, and Lonny does too. Come to think of it, the two of them are looking a little thinner than I remember. Lonny's pa seems specially happy to see Mamma.

He says My Alma How Fine You Are Looking.

Mamma just blushes, like a girl really, like one of those girls who used to chase after Matti.

Thank you Oren, she says.

Pappa tugs at his beard, a sure sign that a storm is brewing.

And Ivan and Alvin and Wendell and Kaarlo and Isaiah and Wilbert and me? Why, we know better than to say anything at all.

Mamma sends Lonny and his pa home with bowlfuls of venison stew and bread and eggs from our hens and cream and even a blackberry pie. They will not be eating tideland grasses for a while from the looks of it.

Pappa is an ornery mood and when I ask him if I can take the little boat out on the Nasel he says, May Amelia, can't you stay out of trouble for two seconds? Girl I swear you are more work than all your brothers put together. You're more trouble than you're worth.

But Pappa— I say. But he is getting all worked up.

You can't take the boat out unless one of the boys is with you, how many times do I hafta tell you May Amelia? I should have just left you in Astoria! he hollers.

I just stand there looking at him and I can see

Pappa thinking I'm gonna run away and hide like I usually do, but he's wrong, I'm never gonna hide again, no matter what. I just stare right back at him and finally he turns in disgust and *Slam!* he's gone out the door.

Nothing's changed, I say.

He's just in a mood, says Wilbert.

He's always in a mood, he hates me, I wish we were back in Astoria.

Wilbert doesn't say anything.

I say, Wilbert take me to the Smith Island, I want to see Baby Amy's marker.

Pappa couldn't afford a fancy marker May, there's only the small cross Isaiah carved, Wilbert says.

I cannot bear the thought of it.

Let's pick some flowers, Wilbert says, but I just shake my head, my heart is too sad for words.

Wilbert picks some daffodils and we row down the Nasel to the Smith Island and walk to the cemetery. It's a fine day and the wind is blowing right off the water, all warm and sweet, not like the day we buried her. When we get to the grave, I feel so sad that she is lying beneath all that dirt that my heart nearly breaks.

I say, Wilbert I am the saddest girl that ever lived.

242

He says, Cheer up May Amelia, Baby Amy is most likely smiling down at us from heaven and she's not sad. Why I reckon she has a pair of wings and all sorts of nice things to eat like we had at Aunt Alice's house.

I am still a very sad girl.

He says, Come on May, the only cure for sadness is a swim in the Nasel.

We decide to head back home and swim upriver from the house, and Bosie comes with us. Bosie's more excited than us children, he loves a swim, he's barking at my feet, and so I undress down to my drawers and dive into the water.

I say, Come On Bosie Jump In Boy.

Old Bosie looks at me once or twice—who can tell what he is thinking—and then without a lick of warning he just jumps right in and starts paddling around.

Well I'll be, says Wilbert. That dog actually minded you.

I say, Come on in Wilbert, the water's fine.

I forgot my sailing boat, Wilbert says, I'll run to the house to get it.

Me and Bosie swim way out to the center of the Nasel and paddle around. Bosie's biting at the water, trying to catch the little fishies.

Bosie, all you're catching is water, I say.

I float on my back and look up at the sky. It's blue as can be and the Nasel water smells so fresh and sweet, like my beautiful Baby Amy. The water tugs and pulls and swirls around me and I think about how I'll never get to teach her to swim or catch fishies on the Baby Island or go to Astoria or have adventures. She is gone forever, deep in the ground. I'll always be the only Jackson girl out here. I will always be alone.

And then, all of a sudden I hear Wilbert screaming and he is running toward us from downriver, running as fast as Matti or Kaarlo even.

Wilbert is hollering and yelling at me, screaming May May Get Outta The Nasel! They're sending the logs downriver, The Dam Is Open Get Out May!

Bosie's yapping beside me, yapping like mad and when I look upriver, sure enough there is something coming downriver in the distance. Huge round logs are rushing down the Nasel from Ben Armstrong's logging camp, rushing straight at us, straight at me and Bosie.

It seems that time slows down to a crawl, and that the wind blowing over the Nasel has never been as sweet, and that the valley has never looked as bright and yellow and crowded with daffodils. And that if I look hard with my heart I

244

can see down the Nasel to the Baby Island and around the bend to my very own snag and farther down to the Smith Island and remember a time not so long ago when I wished myself gone, far away like Baby Amy, far away in heaven with the angels.

And then I look at the bank, at Wilbert waving at me and yelling May May What Are You Waiting For Hurry Up and I know that I'd be very sad indeed if I wasn't around anymore.

I grab Bosie by the piece of rope around his neck and swim as hard as I can to the bank, but the logs are coming fast as salmon. The water is pulling at me and the river is dragging and I can't seem to make my arms move quick enough. I hear the loud rush of the logs banging each other and I think, *I am not going to make it after all,* I am going to be dead and buried with Baby Amy on the Smith Island and it will say on my marker May Amelia Was Not Paying Attention As Usual.

Then all of a sudden I see that Wilbert has climbed the tree on the bank as fast as a monkey, and he swings down from a branch and hoists me up and Bosie too, and when I look down I can't see any water at all only logs crashing down the Nasel. Wilbert pulls me up and we climb down the tree to the ground but I can't catch my breath,

I just sit there dripping wet, Bosie yapping away and shaking and shaking, and Wilbert standing over me, gasping too, and then he grabs my shoulders and shakes me hard, like he can't believe I am sitting here with him on the bank, all covered with mud and whatnot.

I say Wilbert, the Nasel almost got me that time.

He doesn't say anything, just shakes his head, a real GoodLordMayAmelia look on his face.

And I look over his shoulder at the Nasel raging by full of logs, crashing down, the water like an angry waterfall, and imagine Me, May Amelia, lost in that fearsome rush of water, and then I hear Bosie yapping and there are Mamma and Kaarlo and Ivan and Alvin and Isaiah and Wendell and even Pappa running up the bank.

Pappa reaches us first and his face is dark as thunder. I know I'm gonna get a whupping for sure but instead he just pulls me into himself, into a big bear hug. He squeezes the breath right out of me, and when he lets me loose his eyes are all watery.

Oh May, Mamma says.

Wendell, who's still looking frail on account of getting over his fever, is holding Susannah and he

246

says May Amelia We Thought You Were Dead, we thought you were drowned there in the Nasel with all those logs. Didn't you see the boy running by to warn you that they were opening the splash dam?

I shake my head. I did not see any child run by.

He throws Susannah at me.

I just hold Susannah, tight like a baby and look down the river, down the Nasel, to the Smith Island. And I look at Mamma and Pappa and Kaarlo and Wendell and Ivan and Alvin and Isaiah and Wilbert and think of Matti so far away, starting a new life with his Irish bride Mary O'Casey. And I think maybe I am a lucky girl after all, to live here, live on the Nasel, even though it is in the middle of nowhere.

Bosie shakes his fur and barks at me.

I look at Wilbert and say, I am happy to be here Wilbert.

May Amelia, he says on a sigh, I believe we are all quite happy that you are here. After all, you're the only May we've got.

And he was right. I was the only May Amelia Jackson they had.

The first page from the diary of the author's grandaunt,
Alice Amelia Holm.

AUTHOR'S NOTE

Six years ago the diary of my grandaunt, Alice Amelia
Holm, was discovered in an old suitcase in my grandmother's house. As a Christmas present my aunt, Elizabeth
Holm, transcribed the diary and gave copies to family
members. It was one of the best gifts I ever received. The
entries began in 1900, when Aunt Alice was twelve years
old, and ended six years later when she became a teacher.
She wrote about everything from playing tricks on her
brothers to visiting cousins along the river to going fishing. Although Aunt Alice died before I was born, the diary
made me feel as if I knew her—or at least identified with
her. I had always been intrigued by my father's stories
about growing up on the Nasel River, but suddenly I
wanted to know more about my heritage. As I began to
delve into my family's history, I kept imagining what Aunt
Alice's life must have been like—and I started writing what
would become *Our Only May Amelia.*

My great-grandfather Charles Holm emigrated from
Finland in the early 1870s and was one of the first settlers
in the Nasel River Valley. The Washington Territory was
one of the last stretches of unsettled frontier at the turn
of the century. Unlike Oregon, immigration to Washington
did not begin in earnest until the late nineteenth century,
with the boom of the lumber industry in the 1880s and
the completion of the transcontinental railroad in 1893.
The settlers who came to the southwest coast of
Washington, along the Columbia River, were not
Americans from the East who settled in other western

states such as California and Oregon. For the most part they came from Sweden, Norway, and Finland—immigrants lured by the promise of good fishing, timber, and land.

Nasel was settled primarily by Finnish immigrants, and was known locally as Little Finland. However, the Chinook Indians were the first true residents of the Nasel River Valley. "Nasel" comes from the Chinook word *Nasil*, which means sheltered and hidden. A small Indian tribe and their chief were named Nasil, which is how the river came to bear that name. The spelling changed around the end of the nineteenth century to Nasel, and today the river is known as the Naselle.

The Finnish settlers carved out new lives in this harsh wilderness where everything—from chopping down the mighty trees to transporting an iron cookstove—required sweat and ingenuity. The river and swinging bridges were the primary means of transportation until the 1920s, when roads and cars finally became dominant. And like the Jacksons, nearly everyone (including non-Finns) spoke Finnish well into the 1930s. Children typically did not learn English until they began their schooling, which was often sporadic because everyone was needed to help with the farmwork.

In writing this book, I relied heavily upon oral histories from family members as well as local historical societies. I learned that people really did polish the floor with skim milk, eat *laxloda* (which I still eat), and use bear grease and spruce-gum pitch as ointments. The *Gleaner* did sink on the Columbia River during a terrible storm in 1888. The Smith Island, a tideland with a raised knoll on the Nasel River, is named after my granduncles Isaiah Smith and Henry Smith, who homesteaded there in the 1870s. And the May's Snag incident really did happen. Lucy May, a cousin of my grandfather's, was a notoriously chatty girl, and one of her brothers threatened that she would be left on a snag in the river if she didn't stop talking. If you look closely at a detailed map of the Nasel River today, you will find May's Snag, though for the purposes of this story I had to move it closer to the Jackson farm.

And whatever happened to Aunt Alice, my inspiration for May Amelia? She grew up to become a much-beloved teacher in the Nasel area. Her first teaching post, for which she earned $40 a month, was in 1905 on the Smith Island. The last entry in her diary reads:

Feb. 28, 1906

I am a teacher. I studied real hard and passed the exam. . . . Although I think it is nice work, there is so much responsibility about it. . . . I am to begin another term in the Finn country in two weeks & will take this book along so think I'll write some in it there.

Good-bye,
Alice Holm

Glimpses of the Past: Oral Histories from Naselle, by Ruth
  Busse Allingham (South Bend, WA: Pacific
  County Historical Society, 1998).
Remember Where You Started From, by Susan Pakenen
  Holway (Portland, OR: C&D Publishing, 1992).
Fantastically Finnish: Recipes and Traditions, edited by
  Beatrice Ojakangas, John Zug, and Sue Roemig
  (Iowa City, IA: Penfield Press, 1985).
The Pacific County Historical Society in Washington.